A West Point Treasure

Or, Mark Mallory's Strange Find

Upton Sinclair

CONTENTS

CHAPTER I

AN INTERESTING LETTER

"Hey, there, you fellows, I've got a letter to read to you."

He was a tall, handsome lad, with a frank, pleasant face, and a wealth of curly brown hair. He wore a close-fitting gray jacket and trousers. The uniform of a West Point "plebe," as the new cadet is termed. He was standing in front of one of the tents in the summer camp of the corps, and speaking to half a dozen of his classmates.

The six looked up with interest when they heard what he said.

"Come in, Mark," called one of them. "Come in here and read it."

"This is addressed to me," began Mark Mallory, obeying the request and sitting down. "But it's really meant for the whole seven of us. And it's interesting, as showing what the old cadets think of the tricks we bold plebes have been playing on them."

"Who's it from?"

"It's from Wicks Merritt, the second classman I met here last year. He's home on furlough for the summer, but some of the other cadets have written and told him about us, and what we've been doing. And this is what he says about it. Listen.

"Dear Mark: Whenever I sit down to write to you it seems to me I can think of nothing to say, but to marvel at the extraordinary rumpus you have kicked up at West Point. Every time I hear from there you are doing still more incredibly impossible acts, until I expect to hear next that you have been made superintendent or something. However, in this letter I really have something else to tell you about, but I shall put it off to the last and keep you in suspense.

"Well, I hear that, not satisfied with defying the yearlings to haze you, and actually keeping them from doing it, which is something no plebe has ever dared to dream of before, you have gone on to still further recklessness. They say that you have gotten half a dozen other plebes to back you up, and that, to cap the climax, you actually dared to go to one of the hops. Well, I do not know what to say to that; it simply takes my breath away. I should like to have been there to see him doing it. They say that Grace Fuller, the girl you saved from drowning, got all the girls to promise to dance with you, and that the end of the whole business was the yearlings stopped the music and the hop and left in disgust. I fairly gasp when I picture that scene.

"I hesitate to give an original person like you advice. You never heeded what I gave you anyway, but went right ahead in your own contrariness to do what you pleased. I guess you were right. But I want to warn you a little. By your unheard-of daring in going to that hop you have incurred the enmity of not only the yearlings, whom you have beaten at every turn, but also of the powerful first class as well. And they will never stop until they subdue you. I don't know what they'll try, but it will be something desperate, and you must stand the consequences. You'll probably have to take turns fighting every man in the class. When I come back I expect to find you buried six feet deep in court-plaster."

Mark looked up from the letter for a moment, and smiled.

"I wish the dear old chump could see me now," he said.

Wicks' prediction seemed nearly fulfilled. Mark's face was bruised and bandaged; one shoulder was still immovable from a dislocation, and when he moved any other part of himself he did it with a cautious slowness that told of sundry aching joints.

"Yes," growled one of the six listeners, a lad from Texas, with a curious cowboy accent. "Yes, hang it! But I reckon Wicks Merritt didn't have any idea them ole cadets'd pile on to lick you all together. I tell you what, it gits me riled. Jes' because you had the nerve to defy 'em and fight the feller that ordered you off that air hop floor, doggone 'em, they all had to pitch in and beat you."

"Never mind, Texas," laughed Mark, cheerfully. "They were

welcome. I knocked out my man, which was what I went out for. And besides, we managed to outwit them in the end, leaving them deserted and scared to death on the opposite shore of the Hudson. You've heard of clouds with silver linings. I'm off duty and can play the gentleman all day, and not have to turn out and drill like you unfortunate plebes. And, moreover, nobody offers to haze me any more while I'm a cripple."

"It'd be jes' like 'em to," growled Texas.

"That's got nothing to do with the letter," responded Mark. "There is some news in here that'll interest you fellows, if Texas would only stop growling at the cadets long enough to give me a chance. Too much fighting is spoiling your gentle disposition, Texas."

"Ya-as," grinned the Southerner. "You jes' go on."

"I will," continued Mark. "Listen.

"I got a letter from Fischer yesterday. Fischer is captain of your company, I think. He tells me that that rascally Benny Bartlett, the fellow from your town who tried to cheat you out of your appointment, but whom you beat at the examinations, turned up a short while ago with a brand-new plot to get you into trouble. It reads like a fairy story, what Fischer told me. He had a printer's boy hired to accuse you of bribing him to steal for you the exam. papers. The superintendent believed him and you were almost fired.

"Fischer says he went out at night with that wild chum of yours, Texas, and the two of them held up the printer's boy and robbed him of some papers that showed his guilt. Well, Mr. Mallory, I certainly congratulate you on your luck. You owe a debt of gratitude to Fischer, who ought to be your enemy really, since he was one of the hop managers you riled so.

"And now for the news I have. I write to tell you—and I know it will surprise you—that you are not yet through with that troublesome Master Bartlett."

"Wow!" echoed Texas, springing up in surprise. "What does he know 'bout it?"

"Wait," laughed Mark, by way of answer. "Wait, and you'll see. Wicks is quite a detective.

"As you'll notice by the postmark of this letter, I am in Washington, D. C., at present. And what do you think? I have met Benny Bartlett here!

"I can hear you gasp when you read that. I knew him, but he didn't know me, so I made up my mind to have some fun with him. I picked up an acquaintance with him, and told him I was from West Point. Then he got intimate and confidential, said he knew a confounded fresh plebe up there—Mallory, they called him. Well, I said I'd heard of Mallory. And, Mark, I nearly had him wild.

"In the first place, you know, he hates you like poison. I can't tell you how much. This paper wouldn't hold all the names he called you. And, oh, what lies he did tell about you! So I thought to tease him I'd take the other tack. I told him of all your heroism, how you'd saved the life of the daughter of a rich old judge up there, and were engaged to marry her some day. I threw that in for good measure, though they say it is a desperate case between you and her—upon which I congratulate you, for she's a treasure."

"I wonder what he'd say," put in one of the six, "if he knew she'd joined the Banded Seven to help fool the yearlings?"

"I told him," continued Mark, reading, "all about how you'd prevented hazing and were literally running the place. Then I showed him Fischer's letter to cap the climax. And, Mark, the kid was crazy. He vowed he was coming up there to balk you, if it was the last thing he ever did on earth.

"His father has a big pull with the President, and is using it with a vengeance. He pleads that his son did magnificently at the congressman's exams, and only failed at the others because he was ill. And so Benny expects to turn up to annoy you as one of the plebes who come in when camp breaks up on the 28th of August.

"Having warned you of this disagreeable possibility nothing now remains for me to do but wish you the best possible luck in your quarrel with the first class, and so sign myself,

"Sincerely yours,

"Wicks Merritt."

The Seven stared at each other as Mark folded up the letter.

"Fellows," said he, "we've got just one month to wait, just one month. Then that contemptible fellow will be here to bother us. But in the meantime I say we forget about him. He's unpleasant to think about. Let's not mention him again until we see him."

And the Parson echoed, "Yea, by Zeus."

The Parson was just the same old parson he was the day he first struck West Point. Frequent hazings had not robbed him of his quiet and classic dignity; and still more frequent battles with "the enemy" had not made him a whit less learned and studious. He was from Boston, was Parson Stanard, and he was proud of it. Also, he was a geologist of erudition most astoundingly deep. He had a bag of most wonderful fossils hidden away in his tent, fossils with names as long as the Parson's venerable and bony legs in their pale green socks.

The Parson was not wholly devoted to fossils, for he was member No. 3 in our Banded Seven, of which Mark was the leader. No. 4 was "Indian," the fat and gullible and much hazed Joe Smith, of Indianapolis. After him came the merry and handsome Dewey, otherwise known as "B'gee!" the prize story-teller of the crowd. Chauncey, surnamed "the dude," and Sleepy, "the farmer," made up the rest of that bold and valiant band which was notorious for its "B. J.-ness." (B. J., before June, means freshness.)

Master Benjamin Bartlett having been laid on the shelf for a month, the Seven cast about them for a new subject of conversation to while away the half hour of "recreation" allotted to them between the morning's drill and dinner.

"I want to know," suggested Dewey, "what shall we do this afternoon, b'gee?"

That afternoon was Saturday ("the first Saturday we've had for a week," as Dewey sagely informed them, whereat Indian cried out: "Of course! Bless my soul! How could it be otherwise?") Saturday is a half holiday for the cadets.

"I don't know," said Mark. "I hardly think the yearlings'll try any hazing to-day. They're waiting to see what the first class'll do when I get well enough to fight them."

The Parson arose to his feet with dignity.

"It is my purpose," he said, with grave decision, "to undertake an excursion into the mountainous country in back of us, particularly to the portion known as the habitation of the Corous Americanus——"

"The habitation of the what?"

"Of the Corous Americanus. You have probably heard the mountain spoken of as 'Crow's Nest,' but I prefer the other more scientific and accurate name, since there are in America numerous species of crows, some forty-seven in all, I believe."

The six sighed.

"It is my purpose," continued the Parson, blinking solemnly as any wise old owl, "to admire the beauties of the scenery, and also to conduct a little cursory geological investigation in order to——"

"Say," interrupted Texas.

"Well?" inquired the Parson.

"D'you mean you're a-goin' to take a walk?"

"Er—yes," said the Parson, "that is——"

"Let's all go," interrupted Texas. "I'd like to see some o' that there geologizin' o' yourn."

"I shall be delighted to extend you an invitation," said the other, cordially.

And thus it happened that the Banded Seven took a walk back in the mountains that Saturday afternoon. That walk was the most momentous walk that those lads ever had occasion to take.

CHAPTER II

WHAT A WALK LED TO

It was a strangely accoutered cavalcade that set out from this West Point camp an hour or so later. The Parson, as guide and temporary chief, led the way, having his beloved "Dana's Geology" under his arms, and bearing in one hand an "astrology" hammer (as Texas termed it), in the other a capacious bag in which he purposed to carry any interesting specimens he chanced to find. The Parson had brought with him to West Point his professional coat, with huge pockets for that purpose, but being a cadet he was not allowed to wear it.

Chauncey and Indian brought up the rear. Chauncey was picking his way delicately along, fearful of spoiling a beautiful new shine he had just had put on. And Indian was in mortal terror lest some of the ghosts, bears, tramps or snakes which the yearlings had assured him filled the woods, should spring out upon his fat, perspiring little self.

The government property at West Point extends for some four miles up the Hudson, and quite a distance into the wild mountains to the rear. The government property is equivalent to "cadet limits," and so the woods are freely roamed by the venturesome lads on holiday afternoons.

The Parson was never more thoroughly in his element than he was just then. He was a learned professor, escorting a group of patient and willing pupils. The information which he gave out in solid chunks that afternoon would have filled an encyclopædia. A dozen times every hour he would stop and hold forth upon some newly observed object.

But it was when on geology that the Parson was at home. He might dabble in all sciences; in fact, he considered it the duty of a scholar to do so; but geology was his specialty, his own, his pet and paragon. And never did he wax so eloquently as when he was talking of geology, "That science which unravels the mysteries of ages, that reads in the rocks of the present the silent stories of the years that are dead."

"Behold yon towering precipice," he cried, "with its crevices torn by the winter's snows and rains! Gentlemen, I suppose you know that the substances which we call earth and sand are but the result of the ceaseless action of water, which tore it from the mountains and ground it into the ever-moving seas. It was water that carved the mountains from the masses of ancient rock, and water that cut the valleys that lead to the sea below. A wonderful thing is water to the geologist, a strange thing."

"It's a strange thing to a Texan, too," observed the incorrigible cowboy, making a sound like a popping cork.

"This cliff, all covered with vegetation," continued the Parson, gazing up into the air, "has a story to tell also. See that scar running across its surface? In the glacial era, when this valley was a mass of grinding, sliding ice, some great stone caught in the mass plowed that furrow which you see. And perhaps hundreds of miles below here I might find the stone that would fit that mark. That has been done by many a patient scientist."

The six were staring at the cliff in open-mouthed interest.

"In the post-tertiary periods," continued the lecturer, "this Hudson Valley was an inland sea. By that line of colored rock, denoting the top of the strata, I can tell what was the level of that body of water. The storms of that period did great havoc among the rocks. This cliff may have been torn and burrowed; I know of some that had great caves and passageways worn in them."

The six were still staring.

"We find many wonderful fossils in such rock. The seas then were inhabited by many gigantic animals, whose skeletons we find, completely buried in stone. I have the foot of a Megatherium, the foot being about as broad as my arm is long, found in some shistose quartz of this period. If you will excuse me for but a few moments I should like to examine the fragments at the bottom of the cliff and see——"

"I think I see a foot there!" cried Mark, excitedly.

"Where?" demanded the Parson, no less so, his eyes flashing with professional zeal.

"It's the foot of the cliff," responded Mark. "Do you see it?"

The Parson turned away with a grieved look and fell to chipping at the rock. The rest roared with laughter, for which the geologist saw no cause.

"Gentlemen," said he at last, "allow me to remind you of a line from Goldsmith's 'Deserted Village':

"'And the loud laugh that shows the empty mind.'"

Whereupon Dewey muttered an excited "B'gee." Dewey had been so awed by his companion's learning that he hadn't told a story for an hour; but here the temptation was too great.

"B'gee!" he cried. "That reminds me of a story I once heard. There was a fellow had a girl by the name of Auburn. He wanted to write her a love poem, b'gee, and he didn't know how to begin. That poem—the 'Deserted Village'—begins:

"'Sweet Auburn, loveliest village of the plain.'

"So, b'gee, this fellow thought that would do first rate for a starter.

"He wrote to her:

"'Sweet Auburn, loveliest of the plain,' an' b'gee, she wouldn't speak to him for a month!"

Every one joined in the laugh that followed except the Parson; the Parson was still busily chipping rocks with his "astrology" hammer.

"I find nothing," he remarked, hesitatingly. "But I see a most beautiful fern up in that cleft. It is a rhododendron, of the species— —I cannot see it very clearly."

"I'll get it," observed Texas, gayly. "I want to hear the rest of that air name. Don't forget the first part—romeo—romeo what?"

While he was talking Texas had laid hold of the projecting cliff, and with a mighty effort swung himself up on a ledge. Then he raised himself upon his toes and stretched out to get that "rhododendron."

The Parson, gazing up anxiously, saw him lay hold of the plant to pull it off. And then, to his surprise, he heard the Texan give vent to a surprised and excited "Wow!"

"What's the matter?" cried the others.

Texas was too much interested to answer. They saw him seize

hold of a bush that grew above him and raise himself up. Then he pushed aside the plants in front of him and stared curiously.

"What's the matter?" demanded the rest again.

And Texas gazed down at them excitedly.

"Hi, you!" he roared. "Fellers, it's a cave!"

"A cave!" cried the others incredulously.

By way of answer Texas turned, faced the rock again, and shouted a mighty "Hello!"

And to the inexpressible consternation of the crowd an echo, loud and clear, responded:

"Hello!"

It was a cave.

CHAPTER III

MYSTERIES GALORE

The excitement which resulted from Texas' amazing discovery may be imagined. If he had found a "Megatherium," feet and all, there could not have been more interest. Texas was dragged down by the legs, and then there was a wild scramble among the rest, the "invalid" excepted, to see who could get up there first and try the echo.

The entrance, it seemed, was a narrow hole in the rock, completely hidden by a growth of bushes and plants. And the echo! What an amazing echo it was, to be sure! Not only did it answer clearly, but it repeated, and muttered again and again. It took parts of sentences and twisted them about and made the strangest possible combinations of sounds.

"It must be an enormous cave!" cried Mark.

"It has probably fissures to a great distance," observed the geologist. "The freaks of water action are numerous."

"I wonder if there's room for a man to get in," Mark added.

"Ef there ain't," suggested Texas, "we kin force Indian through to make it bigger."

Indian shrank back in horror.

"Ooo!" he cried. "I wouldn't go near it for a fortune. Bless my soul, there may be bears or snakes."

This last suggestion made Dewey, who was then peeping in, drop down in a hurry.

"B'gee!" he gasped. "I hadn't thought of that. And who knows but what a live Megatherium preserved from the tertiary periods may come roaring out?"

"I wish we had a light," said Mark. "Then we might look in and see. I wonder if we couldn't burn that book the Parson has?"

The Parson hugged his beloved "Dana's Geology" in alarm.

"Gentlemen," he said, severely, "I would rather you burned me than this book."

"B'gee!" cried Dewey. "You're most as dry! But a fellow couldn't find a match for you, Parson, if he hunted from now till doomsday."

Parson Stanard turned away with the grieved look he always wore when people got "frivolous." But that mood did not last long; they were all too excited in their strange find to continue joking. They spent half an hour after that peering in cautiously and seeing nothing but blackness. Texas even had the nerve to stick one arm in, at which the rest cried out in horror. Indian's direful hint of snakes or bears had its effect.

It took no small amount of daring to fool about that mysterious black hole. Dewey, ever merry and teasing, was keeping them all on pins and needles by being ceaselessly reminded of grisly yarns. He told of a cave that was full of rattlesnakes, "assorted sizes, all genuine and no two alike, b'gee!" Of another that had been a robber's den with great red-faced, furious, black villains in it, to say nothing of gleaming daggers. Of another, with pitfalls, with water in them and no bottom, "though why the water didn't leak out of where the bottom wasn't, b'gee, I'm not able to say."

It got to be very monotonous by and by, standing about in idleness and curiosity, peeping and wondering what was inside.

"I think it would be a good idea for some one to go in and find out," suggested Mark.

"Bless my soul!" gasped Indian. "I won't, for one."

"And I for two, b'gee!" said Dewey, with especial emphasis.

The rest were just as hasty to decline. One look at that black hole was enough to deter any one. But Mark, getting more and more impatient at the delay, more and more resolved to end that mystery, was slowly making up his mind that he was not going to be deterred. And suddenly he stepped forward.

"Give me a 'boost,'" he said. "I'm going in."

"You!" echoed the six, in a breath. "Your arm!"

"I don't care!" responded he, with decision. "I'm going to find out what's inside, and I'm going to hurry up about it, too."

"Do you mean you're going to crawl through that hole?"

"That's just what I do," he said.

Texas sprang forward with an excited look.

"You ain't!" he cried. "Cuz I'm not going to let you!"

And before Mark could comprehend what he meant his devoted friend had swung himself up to the ledge again, and was already halfway in through the opening.

The others stared up at him anxiously. They saw the Southerner's arms and head vanish, and then, while they waited, prepared for almost anything horrible, they heard an excited exclamation. A moment later the head reappeared.

"Hello!" cried Texas. "Fellers, there's a ladder in thar!"

"A ladder!"

"Yes, sah! That's what I said, a ladder! A rope one!"

Once more the head disappeared; the body followed wriggling. Then with startling suddenness the feet and legs flew in, and an instant afterward, to the horror of the frightened crowd, there was a heavy crash.

Mark made a leap for the opening.

"What's the matter?" he cried.

"Ouch!" they heard the bold Texan growl, his voice sounding hollow and muffled. "The ole ladder busted."

"Ooo!" gasped Indian. "Are you dead?"

Texas did not condescend to answer that.

"Some o' you fellers come in hyar now!" he roared. "I ain't a-goin' to stay alone."

"What's it like in there?" inquired Mark.

"I can't see," answered the other's muffled voice. "Only it's a floor like, an', say, it's got carpet!"

"A carpet!" fairly gasped those outside. "A carpet!"

"I'm going in and see," exclaimed Mark. "Help me up."

The rest "boosted" him with a will. With his one free arm he managed to worm his way through the opening, and then Texas seized him and pulled him through. After that the others followed with alacrity. Even Indian finally got up the "nerve," though loudly bemoaning his fate; he didn't want to come, but it was worse out there all alone in the woods.

Coming in from the brilliant sunlight they were blind as bats. They could not detect the faintest shade of difference in the darkness, and they stood huddled together timidly, not even daring to grope about them.

"Let us remove ourselves further from the light," suggested the Parson, ever learned. "Then we may get used to the darkness, for the retina of the visual organ has the power of accommodating itself to a decrease in intensity of the illuminating— —"

They prepared to obey the suggestion, without waiting for the conclusion of the discourse. But moving in that chasm was indeed a fearful task. In the first place, there were possible wells, so the Parson said, though the presence of the mysterious carpet made that improbable. The first thing Mark had done when he reached bottom was to stoop and verify his friend's amazing statement. And he found that it was just as the other had said. There was carpet, and it was a soft, fine carpet, too.

What that could mean they scarcely dared to think.

"Somebody must live here," whispered Mark. "And they can hardly be honest people, hiding in a place like this."

That did not tend to make the moving about any more pleasant. They caught hold of each other, though there was little comfort in that, for each found that his neighbors were trembling as much as himself. Then, step by step (and very small steps) they advanced, groping in front with their hands, and feeling the ground in front of them with their feet.

"Bless my soul!" gasped Indian. "There might be a trapdoor!"

That grewsome and ghastly suggestion caused so much terror that it stopped all further progress for a minute at least, and when finally they did go on, it was with still more frightened and thumping hearts.

They took two or three more steps ahead; and then suddenly Mark, who was a trifle in the lead, sprang back with a cry.

"What is it?" gasped the rest.

"There's something there," he said. "Something, I don't know what. I touched it!"

They stood in a huddled group, straining their eyes to pierce the darkness. It was horrible to know that something was there, and not to know what. One might imagine anything.

"It's a Megatherium," whispered Dewey, irrepressible even here.

In the suspense that followed the frightened crowd made out that Mark was leaning forward to explore with one hand.

And then suddenly, with a cry of real horror this time, he forced them back hastily.

"It's alive!" he cried.

They were about ready to drop dead with terror by that time, or to scatter and run for their lives. Every one of them was wishing he had never thought of entering this grewsome, black place, with its awful mysteries, its possibilities of fierce beasts or still more fierce and lawless men, or ghosts and goblins, or Heaven only knew what else. Most men do not believe in ghosts or goblins until they get into just some situation like this.

Indian was moaning in terror most appalling, and the rest were in but little better state of mind. And then suddenly the Parson uttered a subdued exclamation. They turned with him and saw what he meant. Facing the darkness as they had, when they turned in the direction of the light that streamed in from the opening, they found that they really could begin to see. But how? The light was so dim and gray that it only made things worse. The seven saw all kinds of horrible shadows about them, above them, beneath them, and not one single object could they distinguish to allay their fears.

Still huddled together, still silent and trembling, they stood and gazed about them, waiting. There was not a sound but the beating of their own hearts until all of a sudden Dewey was heard to whisper.

"B'gee, I've got a match!"

Fumbling in his pockets for a moment he brought that precious object out, while the others crowded about him anxiously. A match! A match! They could hardly believe their ears. Robinson Crusoe never welcomed that tiny object more gratefully.

With fear and trembling Dewey prepared to light it. Every one of them dreaded the moment; horrible though the darkness was, it might be a black shroud for yet more horrible things.

Mark caught him by the arm just as he was in the act of doing it; but it was not for that reason. He suggested that they have papers ready to keep that precious fire going. It was a good idea, and proved so popular that the Parson, filled with a spirit of self-sacrifice, even tore out the blank title pages of his Dana to contribute. And then at last Dewey struck the light.

The match was a good one fortunately. It flickered and sputtered a moment, seeming to hesitate about burning, while the lads gasped in suspense. Then suddenly it flared up brightly, and they gazed about them in dread.

CHAPTER IV

A HORRIBLE DISCOVERY

What a lot of grewsomeness a little match can remove, to be sure! This one did not solve the mysteries of that wondrous cave, but it removed most of the horror of the explorers. It showed, for instance, that the furry thing which Mark had vowed was alive was an ordinary plush-covered chair!

The seven had no time to laugh at that; they were too busy staring. The feeble light could not reach to the other end of the long vista they saw, and neither could one of the papers they hastily lit. But it gave them one glimpse of a most amazing scene.

This cave was indeed a surprising place. The carpet they saw covered nearly all of the floor. There were chairs scattered about, and other articles of furniture. There were some curtains draped from the rocky walls. There were swinging lamps from the vaulted roof. Down in the dim distance there was even a table—a table with shining white dishes upon it. And then the light began to flicker.

Quick as a flash Mark seized it and sprang toward one of the lamps. He was just in time. He whipped off the shade and touched the wick. A moment later they were standing in a brilliant, clear light, that shone to the farthest depths of the place.

The seven bold plebes stood in the center beneath the lamp, perfectly amazed by what they saw. The same idea was flashing across the minds of all of them. This splendor must belong to some one! Those dishes up there were set for a meal! And the owner— where was he? Suppose he should come and find them there? Indian cast a longing glance at the opening that led to freedom outside.

Probably the wisest course for them would have been precipitate flight. To be trapped in there by desperate men would be terrible indeed! But curiosity urged them on. This was a glorious mystery—a mystery worth solving. It was almost a fairy tale; an enchanted princess alone was needed.

Now, whether they would have been bold enough to stay and look about them, had it not been for one occurrence, it is impossible to say. Texas, glancing curiously about him, caught sight of a familiar object on a bench to one side, and he leaped forward and seized it. He stared at it hastily and gave a cry of joy.

It was a revolver! A forty-four calibre, and it was loaded, too!

No power on earth could have moved Texas then; he had a gun; he was at home after that, and he feared neither man nor devil.

"Let 'em come!" he cried. "I'm a-goin' to look."

He strode forward, Mark at his side, and the rest following, peering into every nook and cranny.

One thing seemed certain. There was no one about. The cave had all sorts of passageways and corners, but hunt as they would they saw not a soul, heard not a sound. The place was like a tomb. It was just as silent and weird and uncanny, and moreover just as moldy and dusty as the tomb is supposed to be.

Mark examined the table with its queer outlay of dishes. They were all covered with dust; several had tops, and when Mark lifted them he found that they, too, were empty but for that. It seemed as if dust were everywhere.

Mark was recalled from his interesting exploration by an excited "B'gee!" from Dewey. Dewey was staring at the wall, and as the others ran up to him he pointed without a word in front of him. There was a calendar hanging there. And plain as day, the inscription was still—Tuesday, May the eighteenth, eighteen hundred and forty-eight!

The seven were too mystified by that to say a word. They stared at each other in silence, and then went on.

The next thing to attract their attention was a long workbench at one side. Mark wondered how that thing could ever have come in by the opening, until he saw a box of tools at one side, which suggested that it might have been built inside. There were all sorts of strange looking tools upon the bench, and molds, and dies, and instruments which none of them recognized. Nearby was a forge and a small pair of bellows, a pot of once molten metal, now cold and dust-covered, stood beside it; there were bars, too, of what the puzzled crowd took to be lead.

It was left to the all-wise Parson to discover what this meant. The Parson picked up one of the dies he saw upon the table. He gazed at it curiously, blowing away the dust and cleaning the metal. Then, muttering to himself excitedly, he stepped over to one side of the cave where soft clay was on the floor, and seizing some, pressed it into the mold. He held it before his horrified companions, a perfect image of the United States half dollar; and he spoke but two words of explanation.

"Gentlemen," he said, "counterfeiters!"

The amount of excitement which that caused may be readily imagined. A counterfeiter's den! And they were in it! Texas clutched his revolver the tighter and stared about him warily. As for poor Indian, he simply sat down upon the floor and collapsed.

"Fellows," said Mark at last. "I say we finish examining this place and get out. I don't like it."

None of them did, and they did not hesitate to say so, either. Nothing but curiosity, and the fact that they were ashamed to show their fear, kept them from running for all they were worth. As it was, their advance was timid and hesitating.

They were almost at the end of the cave then. They could see the walls sloping together and the ceiling sloping down toward the floor. The light of the lamp was far away and dim then, and they could not see very clearly. But one thing they did make out to their surprise and alarm. The end of that cave was a heavy iron door, shut tight!

There was but one idea flashed over the minds of every one of the seven at that moment. The money! Here was where the men kept it, in that firmly locked safe.

"B'gee!" muttered Dewey. "I say we go back."

Most of them wanted to, and in a hurry. But there were two of them that didn't mean to; one was the venturesome and reckless Texas, and the other was Mark.

"I'm sorry I came in," said the latter calmly. "But since I'm here I'm going to see the thing to the end. I'm going to search this cave and find out what the whole business means. Who'll help me open that door?"

The Banded Seven weren't timid by a long shot. They had

dared more desperate deeds than any plebes West Point had ever seen. But in this black hole of mystery, suggestive of desperate criminals and no one knew what else, it was no wonder that they hesitated. There was no one but Texas cared to venture near that shadowy door.

Mark himself was by no means as cool as he seemed. He had made up his mind to explore the cave, and he meant to do it, but he chose to hurry all the same. He stepped quickly forward, peering anxiously into the shadows as he did so. And a moment later his hand was upon the door knob.

He shook it vigorously, but found that it was firmly set. It reminded him of the door of a safe, for it had a solid, heavy "feel," and it closed with a spring lock, having no key. Mark noticed that as he was debating with himself whether or not to open it; and then suddenly he gave the knob a mighty wrench and pulled with all his might upon the door.

The knob was rusty, and so were the complicated hinges. The door finally gave way, however, with a creak that was dismal and suggestive. The others shrank back instinctively as the black space it disclosed yawned in front of them.

Mark's heart was beating furiously as he glanced around to peer in. A musty, close odor caught his attention, and then as the faint light made its way in, he saw that beyond was still another compartment, seemingly blacker, and certainly more mysterious than the first. But Mark hesitated not a moment; he had made up his mind to enter and he did. Texas, who was at his back, taking hold of the door to hold it.

Those outside waited for but one moment, a moment of anxious suspense and dread. They had seen their leader's figure vanish, swallowed up in the blackness of the place. They were wondering, tremblingly, as to what the result would be; and then suddenly came a result so terrible and unexpected that it nearly knocked them down. It was a scream, a wild shriek of horror, and it came from Mark!

The six outside gazed at each other, ready to faint from fright; Texas, startled, too, by the weirdness of the tone, sprang back involuntarily. And in an instant the heavy iron door, released from his hand, swung inward and slammed with a dismal clang that rang and echoed down the long, vaulted cave.

The noise was succeeded by a silence that was yet more terrible; not another sound came from Mark, to tell that he was alive or what. And for just an instant, paralyzed with fright, the horror-stricken cadets stood motionless, staring blankly at the glistening door. And then Texas sprang forward to the rescue. He seized the knob furiously, and tearing at the barrier with all his strength, flung it wide open.

"Come on!" he cried. "Follow me!"

Texas was clutching the revolver, a desperate look upon his face; the others, horrified though they were, sprang forward to his side ready to dare anything for the sake of Mark.

But there was no need of their entering. As the light shone in the whole scene was plainly in view. And the six stared with ever-increasing awe. Leaning against the wall, where he had staggered back, was Mark; his face was as white as a sheet; one trembling hand was raised, pointing across the compartment. And the rest followed the direction with their eyes, and then started back in no less horror, their faces even paler than his. Lying flat upon the floor, shining out in the blackness white and distinct and ghastly, their hollow eyes fixed in a death stare upon the roof, were six horrible, grinning skeletons.

Awe-stricken, those reckless plebes stood motionless, gazing upon the scene. They were too dumfounded to say a word, almost to think. And then suddenly, as one man, moved by a single impulse, they faced about and stole silently out of the place. The iron door clanged once more, and then, still silent, the plebes marched in Indian file down the long corridor to where the sunlight streamed in; helped each other out through the narrow opening; and finally, free at last, drew a long breath of inexpressible relief under the clear blue sky of heaven.

It was some minutes after that even before they said a word. Finally Mark spoke.

"Fellows," he said, "there's a mystery. Who can solve it?"

The Parson heaved a sigh and raised his voice.

"There were once," he began, "six counterfeiters, who did their work in a lonely cave. That cave had two entrances, one of which we know of."

"And the other lies at the end of the passageway," said Mark.

"It was a way of escape," went on the Parson, "in case the other entrance was discovered by outsiders. But subsequently that entrance became blocked——"

"And they were caught in their own trap," finished Mark. "That door slammed as it did on me, and they were suffocated. And that is all. Let us go home."

Still awe-stricken and silent, the rest arose and started to follow him. But suddenly Texas, the excitable, irrelevant Texas, stopped and began to gasp.

"Say!" he cried. "Fellers——"

"What is it?"

"D'ye know I never thought of it! That air cave is our'n!"

"How do you mean?"

"There ain't any one else to own it, that's what I mean. An' ef ever we want a place to hide in——"

"Or haze yearlings in," came from Dewey.

"It's ours!" cried Mark. "Just the thing! Hurrah!"

CHAPTER V

A JOKE ON THE PARSON

Mark did not lose any time in telling Grace Fuller all about the cave.

He called on her at the West Point Hotel, where she boarded with her father, and found her sitting on the piazza.

"A real cave!" she cried, with a smile. "How romantic! Have you told — —"

"Nobody but you," said Mark. "It's our secret. We may want to haze some yearlings there, you know. So not a word."

"But you say it was furnished! How wonderful!"

"Yes," said Mark, "even carpets. It seems that this place was once the den of a gang of counterfeiters. I see you open your eyes in surprise. We found all their dies and molds and everything."

"But how do you know they aren't there still?" inquired Grace Fuller in alarm.

"That is the grewsome part of the story. They are all dead. We found that the cave was divided by a heavy iron door. I went into the other part and the door slammed and shut me in. I was scared almost to death, far more than I was the day I swam out to help you. The rest of the fellows opened it at last, and I found that I was shut in with six skeletons. I don't wonder you look horrified. Those criminals had been trapped accidentally in their own cave, just as I was, but they had been suffocated. And there they had lain, we found out afterward, for forty or fifty years."

"It is perfectly terrible!" gasped the girl, her cheeks pale. "I don't see how you will ever dare go into the place again."

"It is a big temptation," laughed Mark. "You see if the cadets continue to try unfair tactics in their efforts to haze us poor unfortunate plebes we can scare some of them into submission up there. And besides, our learned Boston friend, Parson Stanard, has gotten the gold fever. He vows he's going on a treasure hunt in that cave."

"A treasure hunt!"

"Yes. You see it's probable those men had some money, to say nothing of all the bad money they made. And it'll be a case of 'finding's keepings.'"

"I see," said Grace, thoughtfully. And then suddenly she broke into one of her merry, ringing laughs, that compelled Mark to join.

"I think the Parson's such a queer old chap!" she cried. "Isn't he comical? He's so solemn and learned. I can just imagine him prying all about that cave, the same way he does for his fossils."

"I never shall forget the day I first met the Parson," responded Mark. "It was when we were just getting up the Banded Seven to try to stop the hazing. The yearlings had tied his long, bony frame in a sack. He had gotten out and chased the whole crowd of them about the parade ground. And he came into my room in barracks perfectly furious with indignation. Yea, by Zeus!"

"He found out I was interested in geology," said Grace. "I studied it once, and he's never ceased to give me lectures since he found that out. And I never hear anything nowadays but shistose slates, and sandstone conglomerates, and triassic eras, and orohippusses and pertodactyles and brontotheriums."

"He gives us long discourses over in camp, too," laughed Mark. "I can see his lank, bony figure now. It was more comical still when he wore his 'geology coat,' with huge coat tails and pockets for fossils. Anyhow, he gets very much worked up when he's telling us about the glories of geology. And poor Dewey, who's such an inveterate joker, always has to get into trouble by interrupting him. Yesterday, for instance, the Parson was telling us about seashores. He didn't see how any one could fail to appreciate what a wonderful thing a beach was. Here was being written a record that men might read millions of years later. It would be hardened then into imperishable stone. Here, for instance, was the track of a bird. Little by little sand would be scattered over it; more sand on top of that; and so on until it was crushed into rock. That is the way all sandstones are made. Huge convulsions of earth would bring that up to the surface; men would find it, break it open, and there the track of the bird! Wonder of wonders!"

Here Mark paused for breath, and began to laugh.

"What did Dewey say?" inquired Grace.

"He wanted to know if the Parson would classify the summer girl as a bird. He said he'd seen lots of their tracks on the beach. Then he wanted to know if a learned geologist could tell the track of a Chicago girl from that of a Boston girl. Then he went on to imagine the contents of a Coney Island sandstone. The Parson had told of Megatheriums' bones and teeth and skeletons. Dewey wanted to know how about empty sarsaparilla bottles and peanut shells, and tickets to the Turkish dancers and Shoot the Chutes, and popcorn balls, and frankfurters."

"What did the Parson say?" laughed the girl.

"Oh, he just said something about being 'frivolous.' But the climax came a few minutes later when the Parson told how Cavier and other famous scientists had become so wondrously learned that they could tell what an animal was from the tiniest bit of its skeleton, its frame, as he called it. And that started Dewey. He put on his most serious face and told us how he'd read of a great mystery, a geologist who had found the frame of an animal hard as iron, and almost smashed to pieces in some rocks. There was what looked like the body of a man lying near. The first-mentioned thing, so Dewey said, had eighteen teeth in front and seven behind. And the geologist didn't know what on earth it was."

Mark interrupted himself here long enough to indulge in a little silent laughter, and then he went on.

"Well, the Parson took it seriously. He put on his most learned air, and looked it up in 'Dana,' his beloved geological text-book. 'Eighteen in front and seven behind? The rear ones must be molars. Probably, then, it was a Palæothere, but they were extinct before primæval man appears. And it couldn't be one of the Zenglodons, and surely not a Plesiosaurus. Oh, yes! Why, of course, it must be an Ichthyornis!' And the Parson was smiles all over. 'How stupid of that geologist not to have guessed it! An Ichthyornis!' But then Dewey said no, it wasn't. 'Then what is it?' cried the Parson."

"And what did he say?" laughed Grace.

"He said it was a '97 model, seventy-two gear, and the rider had coasted down the hill on it. The teeth weren't molars, they were sprockets. Somebody yelled 'Bicycle!' and the Parson wouldn't speak to him all day."

The girl's merry laughter over the story was pleasant to hear; it was a great deal more pleasant to Mark than the original incident had been.

"I think it's a shame to fool him so," said Grace. "The Parson is so solemn and dignified. And it hurts his feelings."

"He gets over it all," laughed Mark, "and then he enjoys it, too, else we wouldn't do it; for every one of us likes our old geological genius. I don't see what we should do without him. He knows everything under the sun, I'm sure, especially about fossils."

"I don't think it would be possible to fool him," said she.

Mark chuckled softly to himself.

"That remark of yours just reminds me of something else," he said. "The Banded Seven have put up a job to try."

"Try to fool the Parson, you mean?" cried Grace.

By way of answer Mark fumbled under his jacket where the girl had noticed a peculiar lump. He drew forth a bit of stone and handed it to her.

"What would you call that?" he asked.

"It looks for all the world like a fossil," she said.

"Yes," said Mark. "That's what we all thought. Dewey found it, and it fooled him. He thought it was the bone of a Megatherium, or one of those outlandish beasts. We were going to give it to the Parson, only I had the luck to recognize it. It's nothing but a bit of a porcelain jug. And then Dewey suggested that we try it on him, too."

"I should like to see how it goes with the Parson," responded Grace, with a laugh. "I wish you'd try it while I'm around."

The two as they had been talking were gazing across from the piazza in the direction of the summer encampment of the corps. And suddenly the girl gave an exclamation of surprise, as she noticed a tall, long-legged figure leave the camp, and proceed with great strides across the parade ground.

"There he goes now!" cried she.

Mark put his fingers to his lips and gave a shrill whistle. The Parson faced about and stared around anxiously; then, as he saw a handkerchief waving to him from the hotel, he turned and strode in that direction. A minute later his solemn face was gazing up at the two.

"What is it?" he inquired. "I dare not come up there. No, tempt me not. The little volume of instructions designated as the Blue Book denies the pleasure of visiting the hotel without a permit. I fear exceedingly lest I be violating some regulation by standing so near the forbidden ground."

"I'm quite used to getting permits to visit here," laughed Mark. "I think I'll order them by the wholesale soon, that is if Miss Fuller stays much longer.

"I'll bet," Mark added, whispering to the girl, as he noticed the Parson edging off. "I'll bet I can make him break a rule and come up here."

"How?" inquired the girl.

"Parson! Oh, Parson!" cried Mark. "Come up here!"

"Tempt me not!" protested Stanard. "The danger is great and-"

"I've got a fossil to show you," called the other.

The Parson stared incredulously for a moment at the object Mark held up. He suspected a ruse. But no, it was a fossil! And oblivious to duty, danger, demerits and all the rest of the universe, he gave a leap, dashed up the stairs, and fairly pounced upon the two.

"A fossil!" he cried. "By the immortal gods, a fossil! Yea, by Zeus, let me see it."

CHAPTER VI

STANARD'S DEFIANCE

The Parson seemed about ready to devour that "fossil." He seized it and plumped himself down in a chair with a thud. He paused just long enough to deposit his "Dana" upon the floor, and to draw up his learned trousers to the high-water mark, disclosing his pale, sea-green socks. And then with a preliminary "Ahem!" and several blinks he raised the precious relic and stared at it.

The two conspirators were watching him gleefully, occasionally exchanging sly glances. The Parson, all oblivious of this, surveyed one side of the fossil and then turned it over. He tapped it on the arm of his chair; he picked at it with his finger nail; he even tasted it, with scientific public-spiritedness and zeal. And then he cleared his throat solemnly and looked up.

"Gentlemen," said he, "er—that is—ladies—this is a most interesting specimen we have here. I regret that with the brief analysis possible to me I cannot classify it as I should like. A microscopic examination would be undoubtedly essential for that. But some things I can say. This is evidently a fossil bone, a portion of the thigh bone, I should say, probably of some gigantic animal like the Ichthyosaurus. As you will notice from the compactness of the structure and the heaviness, it is much solidified, thus indicating a very remote age, probably the upper Cretaceous at the very least, or possibly the Silurian. I am not able to say positively because——"

The Parson stopped and gazed about him with a surprised and rather injured air. Really the rudeness of some people was amazing! Here were the two he was talking to actually leaning back in their chairs and giving vent to peals of laughter, what about he had no idea. This was really too much!

It was at least five minutes before either Mark or his companion could manage to stop long enough to explain to the puzzled geologist that he had been classifying a porcelain jug. And when they did and he realized it he sat back in his chair and gazed at them in utter consternation. He never said one word for at least a minute; he simply stared, while the idea slowly percolated through his mind. Grace Fuller, ever kind-hearted and considerate, had begun to fear that he was angry, and then suddenly the Boston scholar leaned back in his chair, opened his classic mouth, and forth therefrom came a roar of laughter that made the sentries away over by camp start in alarm.

"Ho, ho, ho!" shouted he. "Ho, ho! ha, ha! he, he! A jug! Yea, by Zeus, a jug! By the nine immortals, a jug!"

Mark stared at him in undisguised amazement. During all his acquaintance with that solemn scholar, he had never seen such an earthquake of a laugh as that. And evidently, too, the Parson was not used to it, for when he stopped he was so out of breath and red in the face that he could hardly move.

And that was the first, last, one and only time that Parson Stanard was ever known to laugh. It took a peculiar sort of a joke to move the Parson.

It took also quite an amount of sputtering and gasping to restore the gentleman's throat and lungs to their ordinary normal condition. That spasm of hilarity which had plowed its way through him like a mighty ship through the waves had left little ripples and gurgles of laughter which bubbled forth occasionally for the next ten minutes at least. It passed, however, at last, to return no more, and Parson Stanard was the same, solemn and learned Parson as ever.

"Gentlemen," said he, "er—that is—ahem—ladies—that was indeed a most extraordinary blunder for a student of geology to make."

"It fooled us all," said Grace, consolingly.

"Ahem!" responded he, with crushing severity. "That was to be expected. But one who has pursued the science as the study of his life should not thus be deceived. Gentlemen, I am tired of being fooled, yea, by Zeus!"

"Do you mean," inquired Mark, "that you want us to stop playing jokes on you?"

Mark had been a little conscience-stricken during that last

prank. He expected the Parson to answer his question in the affirmative, and he meant in all seriousness to agree to stop. But the Parson's answer was different. His professional pride had been awakened.

"I mean nothing of the kind!" said he. "I mean that I no longer mean to let you. I mean that a man who has so long resisted and outwitted our enemy, the yearlings, ought now to be beyond deception. I will no more be fooled!"

There was quite an exciting adventure destined to grow out of that scholarly defiance, an adventure that none of those present had the least suspicion of then.

"Do you mean," inquired Mark, laughingly, "that you defy the Banded Seven to fool you again?"

"Yea, by Zeus!" said the Parson, emphatically. "And I mean not only geologically, but in any other way whatsoever, logically or illogically."

Mark chuckled softly to himself at that.

"I'll try it some day," he said. "I'll give you a chance to forget it meanwhile."

He said nothing more about it then, and a minute or so later the Parson arose to go.

"Ahem!" said he. "Gentlemen—er—that is—ladies—I bid you good-afternoon. I really fear to incur further risk by yielding to the charms of the siren's voice. Farewell!"

Mark and the girl sat in silence and watched his ungainly figure stride away down the path; and suddenly she fell to laughing merrily.

"The Parson's dignity is insulted," she said. "He is getting bold and defiant."

"And I see room for no end of fun just there," responded Mark. "I had an inspiration a few moments ago, watching him. And I have a perfectly fascinating plot already."

"Do you mean," inquired Grace, "that you are going to take his challenge up so soon?"

"That's just what I do," laughed Mark. "I mean to do it this very night, before he's expecting it."

"What is it?"

"I told you a few moments ago, didn't I, that the Parson was excited over the possibility of finding a treasure?"

The girl was staring at Mark with a look of interest and curiosity. That single hint was enough for her quick-witted mind, and her beautiful face was lit up with excitement in a moment.

"Jeminy!" she cried. "That's so! Oo! Let me help, won't you? We'll fool the Parson with a treasure!"

During the next half hour those two conspirators, completely oblivious of everything, just sat and whispered and chuckled. They were off in a lonely corner with no one to overhear them, and they put their heads together and concocted schemes by the bushel, getting more and more excited and hilarious every moment. And then suddenly Mark sprang up with a cry of delight, said good-by in a hurry and rushed away.

"I must tell the rest of the Seven!" he laughed. "This is too good to keep! And oh, say, if we can work it! Whoop!"

CHAPTER VII

STANARD'S STRANGE VISITOR

Dress parade, which took place immediately after the above occupied the time until supper. It was growing dark by the time the battalion marched back from mess hall, and the plebes sighed and realized that one more Saturday half holiday was gone. Parson Stanard, with whom we have to do at present, looked around for his fellow members as soon as the plebe company broke ranks. He found to his surprise that they had disappeared suddenly, gone he knew not where. They had gone to put into execution the plot to fool him, but Stanard did not know it. He turned and strolled away by himself in the gathering dusk.

Near Trophy Point, just west of the camp, stands Battle Monument. North of it stretches one of the finest views that the Hudson Valley affords, a winding river reaching the horizon's end with the mountains of the Highlands sloping to its very shores. The Parson liked that view especially at this "hour of peace." The Parson was wont to preach long sermons to himself upon the sublimity of nature and the insignificance of man, etc., whenever he walked out there. And so now he seated himself in a quiet nook and soon forgot where he was and everything else about himself.

Others knew where he was, however, and from a safe distance were eying his meditative form. It got darker and darker, stars began to come out one by one, and the moon began to turn from white to golden. All this was lost upon the solitary philosopher, who would probably have remained hidden in his own thoughts until tattoo sounded, had it not been for one unpleasant interruption.

Now the Parson did not like to be interrupted; he looked up with an obvious expression of annoyance, when he became aware of the fact that a figure was approaching him, had stopped and was staring at him. But when the Parson surveyed the figure, he forgot to be annoyed, for it was a very peculiar-looking figure, and moreover it was acting very peculiarly too.

From what the Parson could see of him in the darkness he was an old pack peddler. His figure was bent and stooping, and he bore upon his back a heavy load. As to his face, it was so covered by a growth of heavy black hair and beard that the Parson could see nothing but a pair of twinkling eyes. Such was the man; to the Parson's infinite amazement he was setting down his pack and preparing to display his wares to him—to him, the refined and cultured Boston scholar.

"Shoe laces, suspenders?" muttered the curious creature, in a low, disagreeable voice.

"No!" said the other, emphatically.

"Matches, collar buttons?"

"No!" cried the Parson, this time angrily.

"Socks, combs, brushes?"

"No! Go away!"

"Hairpins, needles, necklaces?"

"I tell you I don't want anything!" exclaimed the cadet. "You disturb my meditations, yea, by Zeus, exceedingly! I have no money. I don't want anything!"

The strange old man paid not the least attention to these emphatic and scholarly remonstrances. He was still fumbling at his pack, about to display the contents. And so the Parson, who was exceedingly provoked at having been interrupted in a most valuable train of thought, seeing the man was persistent, sprang up and started to hurry away in disgust.

And then suddenly he was brought to a halt again, completely, as much startled as if he had been shot through the back. For the old man had raised his voice commandingly and called aloud:

"Stop!"

Completely mystified and not a little alarmed by that extraordinary act, the Parson turned and stared at the weird figure. The peddler was still bent half to the ground, but he had flung back his bushy head and extended his hand in a gesture of command.

"Wh—why!" stammered the amazed cadet. "By Zeus!"

The old man continued to stand, his piercing eyes flashing. And then suddenly he dropped his hand and in a low, singsong voice began to mumble, as if to himself. His very first words rooted the Parson to the spot in amazement and horror.

> *"Deep within a mountain dreary*
> *Lies a cavern old and dark;*
> *Where the bones of men lie bleaching*
> *In a chamber, cold and stark."*

The Parson had turned as white as any bones; he was gasping, staring at the horrible creature, who knew the secret that the Parson had thought was his friends' alone to tell. His consternation it is difficult to imagine; the crouching figure saw it, and took advantage of it instantly. Without making another sound, he backed away; beckoning, the Parson following instinctively, helplessly. They stood beneath the protecting shadow of some high bushes, and there once more the weird figure raised his arms, and the amazed cadet quailed and listened:

> *"'Twas a secret not for mortals*
> *Hidden by that cavern walls*
> *For beyond those gloomy portals — —"*

"In the name of all that is holy!" cried the Parson, suddenly. "By the nine Olympians, by the nine Heliconian muses, I abjure you! By the three Cyclos, by the three Centimani, the three Fates, the three Furies, the three Graces! By Acheron and the Styx! By the Pillars of Hercules and the Palladium of Troy. By all that men can mention, yea, by Zeus, I demand to know how you learned this!"

The Parson gasped after that; and the old man went on:

> *"Silence, rash, presumptuous mortal,*
> *Seekest thou the Fates to know?*
> *At whose word e'en Zeus doth tremble,*
> *Sun and earth and moon below."*

There was nothing like a classical allusion to awe the Parson;

convinced of the strange man's superiority, then, he dared not a
word more.

"Bold and reckless those who entered,
Risks they ran they never knew.
But, once entered their's the secret,
Secret that I tell to you.

"At the hour of midnight venture
To that cavern black to go.
Fear not! I protection give thee,
Keep thee safe from every foe.

"Bear a spade upon thy shoulder;
Take thy friends to give thee aid,
Deep to dig in search of treasure
Once beneath its carpet laid.

"Find a lamp—by you 'twas lighted
When you first beheld those halls.
'Tis the secret I shall give thee—
Dig—where'er its shadow falls!"

The old man stopped abruptly. The amazed cadet was staring
at him in the utmost consternation. And then suddenly the man
raised his hand again.

"Go!" he said.

The Parson followed his finger; it was pointing to the camp;
and hesitating but a moment more Stanard turned and started
away, his brain reeling so that he could hardly walk, his ears still
echoing the words:

"'Tis the secret I shall give thee—
Dig—where'er its shadow falls!"

He never once turned to look back at that mysterious figure. If
he had he might have been more surprised than ever. For the

figure, hiding behind the bush, flung off its pack, stepped out of the old man's rags, tore off a heavy false beard and wig and emerged—

Mark Mallory!

He whistled once, and a drum orderly, bribed for the occasion, ran out and hurried off with the things. And Mark rushed over and burst into a group of cadets that stood near.

"It worked! It worked!" he cried. "Oh, you should have seen how it took him in! And he'll go as sure as we're alive."

And just then tattoo sounded and the six villains set out on a run for the camp.

Now Parson Stanard's scholarly features were solemn enough under any circumstances; when there was anything to make them still more so he was a sight to behold. This was the case that evenings for the Parson, when he fell into line, was looking as if the future destiny of the universe were resting upon his shoulders, and his hilarious comrades were scarcely able to keep from bursting into laughter every time they glanced at him.

He was too busy with his own thoughts to notice them, however. He was so much occupied by speculations upon the mystery of that weird old man that he forgot for a moment to answer to his name at roll call, and had to be poked in the ribs to wake him up. Then the line melted away, and still solemn he marched into his tent and gathered his "wondering" fellow-devils about him.

"Gentlemen," said he, "I have a tale to tell you. I have this day, this very hour, met with an adventure, preternatural or supernatural, that exceeds the capacities of the human intellectualities to appreciate. Gentlemen, I am no believer in signs or auguries; but never did the oracle of Delphi or the Sibyl of Cumea promulgate a prophecy more extraordinary than one——"

"What on earth's the matter?" cried the six, in obvious amazement.

"You seen a ghost?" inquired Texas.

"No, gentlemen," said the Parson. "But I have seen some one or something that I should be glad to know was a ghost, something more marvelous than any hitherto recorded, spiritualistic manifestation. And I am sorely perplexed."

After this and a little more of similar introduction the Parson finally managed to get down to business and tell to his horrified (oh, yes!) companions the tale of his adventure.

"Say look a-here, Parson," demanded Texas, when he had finished, "you expect us to believe that aire yarn?"

"That's what I say!" added Mark. "He's trying to fool us."

"Gentlemen," protested the other, "do I look like a man who was joking?"

He didn't for a fact; he looked like a man who had been through a flour mill.

"But that don't make any difference," vowed Mark. "You're just putting on thet face to help deceive us."

"By Zeus!" exclaimed the Parson. "Gentlemen, I swear to you that I am serious. I swear it by the bones of my grandfather. I swear — —"

"Make it grandmother," hinted Texas.

"I swear it by the poisons of Colchia," continued the other indignantly. "By the waters of the Styx, by the sands of the Pactolus, by the spells of Medea, by the thunderbolts of Jove, by the sandals of Mercury — —"

The Parson would probably have continued swearing by everything known to mythology, keeping up until "taps" stopped him. But by that time the conspirators saw fit to believe him.

"This is an extraordinary state of affairs," said Mark, solemnly. "Really, fellows, do you know I think we ought to go?"

"B'gee, so do I," cried Dewey.

"I was about to extend you an invitation," said the Parson. "For my part I am determined to go this very night. Nothing shall stop me, gentlemen. My mind is made up. That treasure, revealed to me under such circumstances, I am determined to secure, and that in spite of whatever dangers I may meet, whatever foes may oppose me, whatever — —"

"Bully for the Parson!" whispered Texas. "He's gittin' spunky."

"We are by no means the first," said the solemn scholar, "to undertake a dangerous search for wealth. The ancient poets sang of Jason and the Argonauts and the Search for the Golden Flecce."

"This yere's the biggest golden 'fleece' of any of 'em," observed Texas, slyly. But the Parson didn't hear that.

He continued all innocent and unsuspecting as ever. And when the Seven went to sleep at last it was with a solemn promise on their lips to be up and doing in time to reach the "cave" by midnight.

As for the Parson, he did not sleep at all; he was too excited. The Parson was in a regular Captain Kidd humor that night. Gold! Gold! He waited impatiently until the "tac" had inspected after taps, and then he turned over on his back and stared at the roof of the tent and lay thinking over the extraordinary adventure he had met with, and the still more extraordinary adventures that were likely to result from it. He was even going so far as to speculate what he was going to do with his wealth. He'd divide it among the rest, of course. And what magnificent fossils he was going to purchase with his share!

He had not long to dwell over that, however. It was two good miles through the woods to that cave, and it might take them some time to find it besides. And not to be there at twelve would be a calamity indeed. The Parson hadn't a very clear idea why he must dig at midnight particularly, but he thought it best to obey orders and ask no questions. So very soon after he heard the sentry call the hour of half-past ten he sprang up and awakened his fellow treasure hunters.

Indian was on guard that night; and so the six remaining who were to conduct the expedition, found no trouble in stealing out of camp. They arose and dressed hastily, and then, not without some little nervousness lest their absence should be noticed, they stole across their friend's sentry beat and made a dash for the woods.

Parson Stanard's gold-hunting expedition was started.

CHAPTER VIII

AN UNEXPECTED RESULT

The walk through that mountain forest was one to be remembered for some time. In the first place, the Parson had been provident enough to fee a drum orderly to steal him a spade and hide it. The Parson insisted upon carrying that spade himself, for that was what the old man had said. And the Parson was careful to carry it upon his shoulder, too. It was surprising how superstitious he had suddenly become; during the dismal trip he enlivened them by a classic discussion of the scientific evidence for and against ghosts, goblins, and magic.

"But, gentlemen," he said solemnly, "one such experience as this of mine convinces a man more than ten thousand arguments, yea, by Zeus!"

Here Texas went into a roar of laughter, which fortunately wound up in a coughing fit and so excited no suspicions.

Did you ever try to walk through a black woods at night—a really dark night? Rocks and logs seem just built to catch your shins; bushes and cobwebs for your eyes. And every one in the party vows that the way they ought to go is off there. The six wandered about desperately, time fairly flying and the excited guide and treasure hunter getting more and more fearful lest the hour should have passed.

It seemed almost by a miracle that they finally reached the cliff in which lay the cave. The entrance was a bush-covered hole in the rocks some ten feet from the ground. The Parson lost not a moment in clambering up and getting in, for he was in a hurry.

The five others, still chuckling joyfully over the success of their deception, followed him in one after another. The party had plenty of matches and candles provided this time, and so one of the lamps in the uncanny place was soon lighted, and then they were ready for work.

The Parson, businesslike and solemn, hauled out his watch.

"Three minutes," he said. "Just in time."

He passed the watch to Mark without another word. Mark held it in his hand to give the signal and the Parson whipped off his coat and seized the shovel with a desperate grip.

"You'll have to cut the carpet," said one of them.

The Parson had thought of that; he hauled a huge clasp knife from under his jacket. Mark considered it a shame to spoil the place that way, and for a moment he thought of telling and stopping the fun. But by that time the thoroughly excited geologist was down on his knees carving out a slice.

He had lit the lamp, according to the directions. Its shadow, of course, fell right underneath, and there the Parson was about to work.

There was a strange scene at that moment, if any one had been there to see it. First there was the mysterious dimly-lit cave; underneath the solitary light stood the excited figure of the long-haired Boston genius, his eyes glittering, his hand trembling. He clutched the spade with determination, and gazed anxiously at Mark, like a racer awaiting the signal. The five others were standing about him, winking at each other slyly, and egging the Parson merrily on. Oh, how they did mean to make him dig!

It was a solemn moment for the Parson. To say nothing of the treasure he meant to find there was his scientific interest in the experiment, testing the old "wizard's" learning. Then suddenly Mark Mallory looked up.

"Now!" said he.

And the Parson jammed his spade into the ground the same instant. The great treasure hunt had begun.

Fairly bubbling over with fun, the conspirators gathered about him, stooping down and staring anxiously, jumping about and exclaiming excitedly, and above all urging the workman to still greater haste.

"Dig! Dig!" they cried.

And you can rest assured the Parson did dig! His long bony arms were flying like a machine. Beads of perspiration gathered on his classic brow; his breath came in gasps that choked off his numerous learned exclamations. And yet he kept on, flinging the dirt in showers about the room until the place began to look as if a sandstorm had struck it. The Parson was working as never had a parson worked before.

The others gave him little chance to rest, either; they kept up his frenzy of excitement by every means they could think of. But such working as that was bound to end soon, for even geological muscles can't stand everything. In this case the end came of its own accord, for the simple reason that the hole got too deep. In his wild excitement Stanard had dug only a narrow one; and by and by he got down so far that he could barely reach the bottom with the end of his shovel. Then he stopped.

"By Zeus!" he gasped, "Gentlemen, this is—outrageous!"

"A shame!" cried Mark. "What are we going to do? Hurry up, it's away after midnight."

The Parson gazed around him wildly; he was as anxious to hurry as any one, but he didn't know what to hurry at.

"Wow!" growled Texas. "Why don't you fellers hurry up thar? Whar's that air treasure? Did you bring me 'way out hyar to git nothin'?"

This and dozens of similar remarks got the Parson very much discouraged and disgusted indeed.

"Gentlemen!" he protested, "I cannot help it, I really cannot! I swear to you by all the inhabitants of Tartæus that if I knew what to do I should do it with all possible celerity. But what——"

"I don't believe there's any treasure there," growled Texas. "It's all a fake."

"That's what I say, too, b'gee!" cried Dewey. "I just believe the Parson wanted to show us he knew how to dig graves. I wish I were asleep in my tent! Reminds me of a story I once heard, b'gee-"

"Don't tell us any stories," exclaimed Mark with feigned anger. "The Parson has told us enough for one night. This is outrageous."

The poor Parson had sunk into a chair in exhaustion and resignation. Evidently there was no more fun to be gotten out of him, Mark thought, and was about to propose returning to camp, when suddenly another idea flashed across him.

"Jove!" he exclaimed, excitedly. "I didn't think of that!"

The Parson sprang up again with a sudden renewal of interest and life.

"What is it?" he cried. "What is it?"

"I've got an idea!" shouted Mark. "Ye gods! Why didn't I think of that before. I know why we haven't found the treasure!"

The Parson's excitement was genuine; the others joined in with his exclamations to keep up the effect.

"What is it?" they cried, yet more loudly.

"Did that wizard tell you to light the lamp?" Mark demanded of the Parson.

"N—no," stammered the other, obviously puzzled, "but how else could it have a shadow?"

For an answer Mark sprang forward and extinguished the lamp. Then he turned and cried triumphantly:

"Look!"

In the partial darkness the light of the moon, coming in through the hole, alone was visible. It struck the lamp right full and cast a deep black shadow over in one corner of the cave, close to the wall.

"Ha!" exclaimed Mark dramatically. "There's the spot!"

"B'gee!" cried Dewey, falling in with the scheme. "So it is! And that's why he told you to dig at midnight, b'gee!"

Already the Parson had seized his spade and made a regular kangaroo leap for the place. Before his hilarious comrades could even start to follow he had broken ground once more and was flinging the dirt about with even more reckless eagerness.

"Go it, go it!" roared the rest.

The crowd gathered about him in a circle, clapping their hands, dancing about, and shouting like "rooters" at a baseball game in the oft-quoted case of "the ninth inning, two out, score a tie," etc. And never did a batter "lam her out" with more vigor than the treasure-hunting scholar "lammed her" into that ground.

They reached the two-foot mark, and then began the same trouble of inability to reach the bottom.

"Better make it bigger, b'gee," laughed Dewey. "Don't give up. If it don't work this time, b'gee, we'll light every other lamp in the place and try their shadows. And then——"

And then with an exclamation of excitement the Parson sprang back.

"I've struck something!" he cried.

"Whoop!" roared the crowd chuckling. "We've found the treasure! Hooray!"

"It's hard," panted the excited Stanard.

"It's as hard as a rock, isn't it?" said Mark, with a sly wink. And then he added under his breath, "A rock it is."

But the Parson was too busy to hear that. He was working feverishly, plunging his spade into the ground, flinging out the earth, occasionally hitting the object with a sharp sound that made him get more overjoyed and the rest get more convulsed with laughter.

Truly the solemn Parson digging a trench was a most ludicrous sight; his next move was more ludicrous still. He got down on his stomach, flat, and reached into the ground.

"Whoop!" roared Texas, "it's good he's got long arms! Hooray, we've got our treasure!"

"Yes, by Zeus!" cried the Parson, springing up and facing them. His next words almost took them off their feet, and no wonder. "Gentlemen," he said, solemnly, "we have got a treasure! It's got a handle!"

The five stared at each other in dumb amazement.

"A handle!" they echoed. "A handle!"

And then Mark flung himself to the ground, and reached in.

When he got up again it was with a look on his face that struck the others into a heap.

"Fellows," he cried, "as I live, it has got a handle!"

The Parson of course was not in the least surprised; it was what he had been expecting all along. What surprised him was their surprise, and incredulity, and blank amazement. Each one of them must needs stoop and verify Mark's extraordinary statement, learn that there was something down there with a handle for a fact. And then, as completely subdued and serious as ever were merry jokers they took the spade from the exhausted Stanard and set to work to dig with real earnestness, and in silence. No exclamation they could think of came anywhere near expressing their state of mind.

They widened the hole the Parson had made, and thus exposed one corner of the object, which proved to be a wooden chest, of what size they could not tell. And that discovery completed the indescribable consternation of the five. There never was a joke stopped much more abruptly than that one.

They continued digging; to make a long story short they dug for half an hour steadily, and by that time had succeeded in disclosing the box which was over two feet long and surrounded by hard clay. Having freed it, Mark sprang down and tried to life it; he failed, and they dug the hole yet wider still. Then, fairly burning up with excitement and curiosity and eagerness, the whole five got down into the ditch and lifted out the chest.

It cost them quite an effort even then; but they got it out at last and gathered around it, staring curiously, whispering anxiously. It was locked firmly, that they could see. But the wood was rotten and Mark seized the shovel and knocked the hinges off the back with one quick blow. Then the six stood and stared at each other, each one of them hesitating for a moment before revealing that uncanny mystery.

That did not last very long, however. Mark grasped the lid firmly and wrenched it back. And as one man the six leaped forward to glance in.

"Gold!"

The cry burst from throats of every one of them at once. They sprang back and gazed at each other in amazement. For that huge chest was fairly brimming over with five-dollar gold pieces!

Oh, what a scene there was for the next ten minutes. The cadets were fairly wild. They stooped and gazed at the treasure greedily. They ran their fingers through it incredulously; they danced about the cave in the wildest jubilation. For there was in that chest money enough to make each one of them rich.

And then suddenly an idea flashed over Mark. This was a counterfeiter's cave!

"Is it genuine?" he cried.

Quick as a wink the Parson whipped two bottles from under his coat.

"I thought of that," he said. "Yea, by Zeus! One is for gold, one silver."

He wrenched the stopper out of one bottle and stopped eagerly, the seven staring in horror.

"If it's gold," he cried, "it'll turn green!"

He snatched up one, and poured the acid over it. And the six broke into a wild cheer as they saw the color come.

"Try another!" cried Mark.

For answer the Parson sprang forward and poured the contents of the bottle over the coins. Everywhere it touched the tarnished metal it showed the reaction. And the six locked arms and did a war dance about the place.

"We're rich!" they cried. "We're rich!"

And then they stole back to camp again.

CHAPTER IX

DISCOVERY OF THE LOSS

"This is where you wake up and find yourself rich; how do you like it?"

Mark, who asked the question, was yawning sleepily as he sat up from his bed, a pile of blankets on the floor of his tent. It was about five o'clock Sunday morning, and the booming echo of the réveille gun was still upon the air. Down by the color line a drum was still rattling, with a fife to keep it company. And throughout the camp cadets were springing up to dress, just as were the four we noticed.

There is no tent room in West Point for the man who likes to lie in bed and doze for half an hour in the morning; cadets have five minutes to dress in, and they have to be out in the company street lined up for roll call at the end of that time. And there is no danger of their failing about it, either. They tell a good story up there about one fond mother who introduced her young hopeful, a soon-to-be plebe, to the commandant of cadets, and hoped that they wouldn't have any trouble getting "Montmorency dear" up in the morning; they never could get him up at home.

But to return to the four A Company plebes who were meanwhile flinging on their clothes and performing their hasty toilets.

The lad who propounded the question was Mark, as said before. The one who answered it was Jeremiah Powers, and Texas vowed he liked being rich mighty well. He got no chance to explain why or wherefore, however, for by that time he was outside of the tent, and the resplendent cadet officer was giving his stentorian order:

"'Tenshun, company!"

At which signal the merry groups of cadets changed into an immovable line of figures stiff as ramrods.

The plebes had come back to camp late last night, or rather

early this same morning, scarcely able to realize what had happened. They were still striving to realize it all as they sat whispering to each other in mess hall. They were rich, all of them. How much they had none of them had any idea. The learned Parson had informed them—and he didn't have to go to a book to find it out, either, that a pound of gold is worth two hundred and fifty dollars. Allowing two hundred pounds to that box, which was a modest guess indeed, left some seven thousand dollars to each of them, a truly enormous fortune for a boy, especially a West Point plebe who is supposed to have no use for money at all.

Cadets do their purchasing on "check-book," as it is called, and their bills are deducted from their salaries. And though they do smuggle in some contraband bills occasionally they have no way of making use of large sums. This was the problem the Banded Seven were discussing through the meal and while they were busily sprucing up their tents for "Sunday morning inspection."

Texas was for quitting "the ole place" at a jump and making for the plains where a fellow could have a little fun when he wanted to. The fact that he had signed an "engagement for service," or any such trifle as that, made no difference to him, and in fact there is little doubt that he would have skipped that morning had it not been for one fact—he couldn't leave Mark.

"Doggone his boots!" growled Texas, "ef he had any nerve he'd come along! But ef he won't, I s'pose I got to let that air money lie idle."

After which disconsolate observation Texas fell to polishing the mirror that hung on his tent pole and said nothing more.

"Think of Texas running away!" laughed Mark. "Think of him not having Corporal Jasper to come in on Sunday mornings and lecture him for talking too much instead of sprucing up his tent as a cadet should. Think of his not having Captain Fisher to march him 'round to church after that and civilize him! Think of the yearlings having nobody to lick 'em any more! Think of Bull Harris, our beloved enemy, who hates us worse than I do warm cod liver oil, having nobody to fool him every once in a while and get him wild!"

Mark observed by that time from the twitching in his excitable friend's fingers and the light that danced in his eye that his last hit had drawn blood. Texas was cured in a moment of all desire to leave West Point. For was not Bull Harris, "that ole coyote of a yearlin'," a low, cowardly rascal who had tried every contemptible trick upon Mark that his ingenuity could invent, and who hadn't had half his malignity and envy knocked out of him yet? And Texas go away? Not much!

Parson Stanard was heard from next. The Parson knew of a most extraordinary collection of fossils from the Subcarboniferous period. The Parson had been saving up for a year to buy those fossils, and now he meant to do it. He swore it by Zeus, and by Apollo, and by each one of the "Olympians" in turn. Also the Parson meant to do something handsome by that wonderful Cyathophylloid coral found by him in a sandstone of Tertiary origin. The Parson thought it would be a good idea to get up a little pamphlet on that most marvelous specimen, a pamphlet treating very learnedly upon the "distribution of the Cyathophylloid according to previous geological investigations and the probable revolutionary and monumental effects of the new modifications thereof." The Parson had an idea he'd have a high old time writing that treatise.

Further discourse as to the probable uses of the treasure was cut short by the entrance of the inspecting officer, who scattered slaughter and trembling from his eye. Methusalem Z. Chilvers, "the farmer," alias Sleepy, the fourth occupant of the tent, was responsible for disorder that week and the way he caught it was heartrending. He was so disgusted that as usual he vowed he was going to take his money back to Kansas and raise "craps." After which the drum sounded and they all marched down to chapel.

A delightful feeling of independence comes with knowing you are rich. Perhaps you have never tried it, but the Seven were trying it just then. They beamed down contentedly on irate cadet corporals and unfriendly yearlings with an air of conscious superiority that seemed to say, "If you only knew." Of the Seven there were only two who were at all used to the sensation of being wealthy. Texas' "dad," "the Honorable Scrap Powers, o' Hurricane County," owned a few hundred thousand head of cattle, and Chauncey, "the dude," was a millionaire from New York; but all the others were quite poor. Mark was calculating just then what a satisfaction he meant to have in sending some of that money to his widowed mother, to whom it would be a very welcome present indeed.

He was thinking of that in the course of the afternoon, when church and likewise dinner had passed, leaving the plebes at leisure. And so he proposed to them that they take a walk to pass the time and incidentally bring some of that buried wealth back with them. Nothing could have suited the Seven better, as it happened. They were all anxiety again to get up to that cave and hear those gold coins jingle once more. To cut the story short, they went.

It was a merry party that set out through the woods that afternoon. The Seven were usually merry, as we know, but they had extra causes just then. Everything was going about as well for them as things in the world could be expected to go. And besides this, Parson Stanard, who was a wellspring of fun at all times, was in one of his most solemn and therefore laughable moods at present.

The thought had occurred to the Parson, as his first sordid flush of delight at having wealth had passed, that after all he was in a very unscholarly condition indeed. The very idea of a man of learning being rich! Why it was preposterous; where was all the starving in garrets of genius and the pinching poverty that was always the fate of the true patrons of Minerva. That worried the Parson more than you can imagine; he felt himself a traitor to his chosen profession. And with much solemn abjurgation and considerable classical circumlocution he called the Seven's attention to that deplorable state of affairs. Search the records of history as he could, the Parson could not find a parallel for his own unfortunate condition. And he wound up the afternoon's discussion by wishing, yea, by Zeus, that he could be poor and happy once more.

Dewey suggested very solemnly that nobody was going to compel the unfortunate Parson to claim his share, "b'gee"; that he (Dewey) would be pleased to take it if he were only paid enough to make it worth while. But somehow or other the Parson didn't fall into that plan very readily; perhaps he didn't think Dewey really meant it.

Still chatting merrily, the Seven made their way through the mile or two of woods that lay between the post and the cave.

As they drew near to the opening the plebes were startled to notice that the ground at the foot of the rock was marked and torn with footprints.

The Seven had not done that, they knew, for they had been of all things most careful to leave not the least trace that should lead any one to suspect the presence of their secret cavern. And consequently when they saw the state of the ground there was but one thought, a horrible thought that flashed over every one of them. Somebody had been in their cave! And during the night!

Almost as one man, the Seven made a dash for the entrance, scrambling up the rocks. There was never a thought of danger in the mind of any one of them, never a thought that perhaps some accomplice of the dead counterfeiters had come to get the gold, might now be inside, armed against the intruders. They had time to think of but one thing. Somebody had seen them go in last night, had seen them find the treasure! And now—and now?

Texas was the first of them to get to the entrance, for Mark was still lame with his injured arm. He flung his body through the hole, half falling to the floor on the other side. The rest heard him stumbling about and they halted, silent, every one of them, scarcely breathing for anxiety and suspense. They heard Texas strike a match. They heard him run across the floor— —

And a moment later came a cry that struck them almost dumb with horror.

"Boys, the money's all gone!"

CHAPTER X

DISCOVERY OF THE THIEF

The state of mind of the Seven cannot be described. A moment before they had been upon a pinnacle of success and happiness. And now it seemed that they had climbed but that their fall might be all the more unbearable. All their ambitions and plans, all the fun they meant to have—it was too terrible to be true!

It was half with a feeling of incredulity that one after another they climbed up to the opening and went in. Not one of them could quite bring himself to believe that the whole thing was not a horrible delusion, a nightmare. But when they got inside they found that it was too true.

There was the deep trench that Parson Stanard had dug; there was the spade he had dug it with, the tracks of the others who had gathered anxiously about to watch him. There was even one of the bright glittering gold pieces half hidden in the dirt, a horrible mockery, as it appeared to them; for the big wooden chest that had been full to the brim with gold pieces, was gone, and the money with it. And all the hopes of the Banded Seven were gone, too.

At first they stood and stared, gasping; and then they gazed about the place in horror, thinking that surely they they must find the chest lying somewhere else. But it was not there. They dashed around the room, hunting in every corner of the place, even in the locked cell, where the ghastly skeletons lay grinning at them as if in delight. But there was not a sign of the chest, nor of any one who could have taken it.

And then suddenly Mark noticed a footprint in the soft earth just underneath the entrance that told him the story.

"They've taken it out!" he cried.

Feverish with disappointment and impatience, the Seven scrambled out again through the hole. There on the ground was the same footprint, larger than any of theirs. It did not take half an eye to see that. There, too, was a great three-cornered dent in the ground, showing where the chest had been dropped. And there were finger marks of the hand that had scooped up the fallen coins to put them back into the chest.

Texas, plainsman and cowboy, had often told stories of how he had followed a half-washed out trail for miles across an otherwise trackless prairie. He was on his knees now studying every mark and sign, his eyes fairly starting from his head with excitement. And suddenly he sprang to his feet as he noticed a trail a short way off, a deep, smooth rut worn in the earth.

"A wheelbarrow!" roared he.

A wheelbarrow it was, for a fact. And the track of it lay through the woods to the river. Texas had started on a run, without saying another word, and the rest were at his heels.

The men who had taken that heavy chest down that steep forest slope to the river must have had hard work. Any one could see that as he looked at the mark of the wheel. It would run down a slippery rock and plunge deep into the soft earth at the bottom. It would run into a fallen log, or plunge through a heavy thicket. And once, plain as day was written a story of how the chest had fallen off and the heap of scattered coins all been gathered up again.

These things the plebes barely noticed in their haste. They ran almost all the way. It was perhaps two hundred yards to the river, and there was a steep, shelving bank, at the bottom of which was a little pebbly beach. Down the bank the wheelbarrow had evidently been run, half falling, upsetting the box once more, and necessitating the same labor of gathering up the coins. One of them had been left in the sand.

The poor plebes realized then how hopeless was their search. Deep in the sand was the mark of a boat's keel, and they knew that the work of trailing was at an end. Their treasure was gone forever, stolen during the few hours since they had left it last.

"There's no use shedding any tears about it," said Mark at last, when the state of affairs had had time to be realized. "We've simply got it to bear. Somebody probably saw us leave the camp last night and followed us up here. And when they saw that treasure they just helped themselves."

There is little that will make most people madder than to be told "never mind" when they feel they have something to be very much worried over. The Seven did mind a great deal. They sat and stared at each other with looks of disgust. Even the Parson (who ought to have been happy) wore a funereal look, and the only one who had a natural expression was Indian, the fat boy from Indianapolis. That was because Indian looked horrified and lugubrious always.

They wandered disconsolately about the spot where the boat had landed for perhaps five minutes, gazing longingly at the trace of the boat in the sand and wishing they could see it in the water as well, before any new development came. But the development was a startling one when it came. It took no detective to read the secret; it was written plain as day to all eyes in an object that lay on the ground.

Mark was the first to notice it. He saw a gleam of metal in the sand, and he thought it was one of the coins. But a moment later he saw that it was not, and he sprang forward, trembling with eagerness and sudden hope.

A moment later he held up before his startled companions a handsome gold watch. They sprang forward to look at it. Crying out in surprise as they did so, and a moment later he turned it quickly over. Written upon the back were three letters in the shape of a monogram—a monogram they had seen before on clothing, worn by a yearling, and that yearling was— —

"Bull Harris!"

The scene that followed then precludes description. The Seven danced about on the sand, fairly howled for what was joy at one moment, anger at another. There was joy that they had found a clew, that they knew where to hunt for their treasure; and anger at that latest of the many contemptible tricks that yearling had tried.

What Bull Harris had done scarcely needs to be mentioned here—at least, not to old readers of this series. He had tried every scheme that his revengeful cunning could suggest to even matters with that hated Mark Mallory. He had tried a dozen plans to get Mark expelled, a dozen to get him brutally hazed. And they had all been cowardly tricks in which the yearling took good care to run no danger. This was the last, the climax; he had stolen their treasure by night, and what was almost as bad had he found their secret cavern. And as Mark stood and stared at that watch he clutched in his hand he registered a vow that Bull Harris should be paid for his acts in a way that he would not forget if he lived a thousand years.

And then he turned to the others.

"Come on, fellows," he said. "We can't gain anything by standing here. Let's go back and watch Bull Harris like so many cats until we find out what he's done with our money."

The Seven turned and made their way through the woods once more, talking over the situation and their own course as they went. They had room for but one idea in their heads just now. They must find out where that money was and get it back, if it was the last thing they ever did in their lives.

It was clear that the hiding place could not be very far away, and that Bull and his cronies must go to it again. The Seven had left the place at about one in the morning, and réveille came at five; that gave but four hours in which Bull, who it was presumed, had watched them digging, had returned to West Point, gotten a boat and wheelbarrow and taken the treasure away. He could not have taken it a great distance in that time.

Another question was, who had helped him? Probably some of his gang, Mark thought, until he chanced to remember that Bull had another ally just then. He had a cousin, a youth even less lovely than he staying at the hotel. And then came another vague idea— perhaps he had the treasure there. Bull could surely not have it in his tent, and perhaps he had been afraid to bury it.

That was but a faint hope, yet Mark decided in a moment to follow it up. He thought of a scheme. Grace Fuller was at the hotel, and also George, the Fuller's family butler. George was a merry, red-faced Irishman, who had once fired off some cannon at night for the plebes and scared West Point out of its boots. Mark determined after a moment's consultation that George was the man to investigate this clew for them.

As I said, it was only a possibility, a very bare one. Mark strolled around near the hotel late in the afternoon when he returned, keeping a sharp lookout for the man just mentioned. When he saw him he whispered to him and strolled slowly away.

"George," said Mark, hurriedly, when the other joined him, "do you know which is Cadet Harris' cousin, the young man who's staying in the hotel there?"

"Yes, sir," said the butler. "His name's Mr. Chandler. Why?"

"I've got a secret," said Mark, briefly. "It's something important, and I want you to help me, without saying a word to any one. Get one of the women, his chamber-maid if you can, to find out if he's got a box in his room."

And the butler chuckled to himself.

"Bless you, sir," he said. "I can tell you that now. It's the talk of the place, among the help. One of the girls saw Mr. Harris and his cousin carrying a heavy box up to his room just before réveille this morning."

And as Mark turned away again he was ready to shout aloud for joy.

CHAPTER XI

STEALING FROM THIEVES

"Now," said Mark, when he rejoined his companions, "we've got pretty definite information to go on with now. Mr. Chandler's got our money in his room. The question is what are we to do next?"

The plebes were sitting over in a secluded corner of Trophy Point discussing this. Texas doubled up his fists with an angry exclamation.

"Git it back!" growled he, with a characteristic disregard of details.

"But how?" said Mark. "Of course we could have him arrested, for he knew the money was ours. But if we did he'd tell how we skipped camp to dig it and we'd be dismissed from West Point. Then there'd be the old Nick to pay."

"One case where I'd be thankful I'm not in the habit of paying my debts," observed Dewey, tacking on a stray "b'gee" as usual. "As to Bull and his cousin, I say we punch their faces till they give up the money. Punch their faces, b'gee!"

"Doggone their boots!" growled Texas.

"That might hurt their boots," laughed Mark, "but it wouldn't do us any good. I haven't heard any feasible suggestion yet. You know possession is nine points, and they've got that."

It was Mark who finally hit upon a plan that seemed possible. It was a wild and woolly plan, too, and it took Texas with a rush.

"They stole it from us," said Mark. "I don't see what better we can do than steal it back again."

"You don't mean— —" gasped Dewey—"b'gee— —"

"Yes, I do," laughed Mark. "And I mean this very night, too. I mean that we turn burglars and get our money out of there."

And Mr. Jeremiah Powers let out a whoop just then that made the windows rattle over in that selfsame hotel. Jeremiah Powers hadn't been quite so excited since the time he rode out and tried to hold up the cadet battalion. When the others assented to the plan and vowed their aid, he nearly had a fit.

After that the Seven did almost nothing but glance at their watches during the fast-waning Sunday afternoon. There was no parade to pass the time. It seemed an age between the sunset gun and supper; and as for tattoo, all the Parson's much-vaunted geologic periods, times, ages and eras, Silurian, Devonian, Carboniferous, Treassic, Jurassic and Cretaceous, were not to be compared with it in length. When they did finally get into bed they waited another age for taps to sound, and another for the tac to inspect, and another till the sentry called half-past ten, and another for eleven, and another for half-past that, and then twelve, and they couldn't stand it any longer.

No matter if it was a rather early hour for burglars to begin operations, they could not wait any longer. Not a man of them had gone to sleep (except Indian), such was their impatience. They got up, all of them, and began to dress hastily, putting on some old clothes a drum orderly had smuggled in. And a few minutes later that momentous expedition crossed the sentry post unseen and sat down in old Fort Clinton.

Nobody means to say for a moment that there was one of them who was not badly scared just then. None of them was used to playing burglar and they could not but see that it was a very serious and dangerous business at best. Old hands at it often get into serious scrapes, so what shall we say of greenhorns? The only one of them who had ever "done a job" was Texas, who had once gotten Mark out of a bad scrape that way.

They discussed the programme they were to follow. They knew where the room was and that it could be reached by climbing the piazza pillars to the roof above. Texas had climbed those pillars once before, and he had a rope to help Mark and the rest up this time. After that they were to enter that room, and Texas, the desperate cowboy, was to hold young Chandler up till the deed was done. That was all, very simple. But, oh, how they shivered!

They were ugly enough looking fellows externally. The clothes they wore were old and tough-looking, turned up at the collars. Mark had in his free hand a dark lantern, and Texas was clutching in his pocket a heavy forty-four caliber which he meant to use. They had masks, every one of them, or such masks as they could make out of their handkerchiefs. And anybody who saw them stealing across the grass to the hotel grounds would have been very much alarmed indeed.

Fortunately it was a cloudy night, black as pitch.

Even the white trousers of the lonely sentries who paced the walks about the camp were scarcely distinguishable. The hotel was a black, indistinct mass looming up in front of them. The chances of recognition under such circumstances were few, the plebes realized with a sense of relief.

Once hiding close under the shadow of the building they wasted but little time in consultation. It was a creepy sort of business altogether, but then they had started, and so there was nothing to do but go right ahead. Most of them had recovered from their first nervousness at this crisis anyway, of course excepting poor Indian, who had seated himself flat on the ground in a state of collapse. Dewey was behind him ready to grab him by the mouth in case one of Indian's now famous howls of terror should show any signs of breaking loose.

Texas and Mark meanwhile were proceeding calmly to business. The pillars were very wide and high, and Mark foresaw trouble in getting himself up them with his crippled arm. And there was still more trouble in the case of the gentleman from Indianapolis, whose fat little legs wouldn't reach halfway around. The difficulty was fortunately removed by the finding of a short ladder in back of the house. A very few minutes later the seven anxious plebes were lying upon the piazza roof.

They wormed their way up close to the wall of the building where they were safe from observation. And while Mark devoted himself to keeping Indian quiet Texas set out to reconnoiter. Poor Indian didn't want to come, and worse yet, he didn't want to stay. He felt safer in the hotel as a burglar than all alone outside in the darkness, and he had an idea that even Camp McPherson wasn't safe without Mark. "Alas, poor Indian!"

Meanwhile as to Texas. Did you ever walk on a tin roof? If you have you can imagine what a soul-stirring, ear-splitting operation it is, at midnight, especially when you are in burglar's costume, with a revolver in one hand and a dark lantern in the other. Every single individual bit of tin on the flooring seemed to have a new and original kind of sound to make, and the six watchers quailed at every one of them.

Texas was hunting for the window that led into the hall of the building. The room they meant to enter was unfortunately on the other side. They had to force the window, creep down the hall and get into that room. If they could simply have entered it from a window, they might have gotten out of this foolish scrape a good deal more simply than they did.

Texas managed to locate the window without much trouble, and fortunately he found it open. He beckoned the others silently, and they crept one by one down to the place, Indian making twice as much noise as any one because he weighed more. At any rate they climbed through the window and into the lonely hall of the hotel, where they stood and listened anxiously. They had not been very quiet, but they did not believe they had awakened any one; and after this they could be quieter.

They would have been very much scared and terrified plebes, more so, all of them, than was Master Smith now, if they could have known the true state of affairs. For they had awakened some one. And though they had not the least suspicion of it, a pair of sharp eyes had been watching their every move.

They were very beautiful eyes, too. They belonged to a young girl, a girl with lovely features and bright golden hair. She was sleeping in one of the rooms on the second floor that fronted on the piazza, and the sound that awakened her had been the gentle tap upon the roof when the ladder had been raised. She sat up in bed, and a moment later arose and crept tremblingly to the window. Peering out into the darkness she saw the top of the ladder, and a moment later saw a masked face appear above it, and a masked figure climb up and creep into the shadow of the building. Another followed it instantly, and another; and then without a sound the girl dodged down and stole across the floor of the room.

She crept silently to a trunk that was in one corner; she raised the lid and fumbled about anxiously in the darkness for something.

It felt cold, like polished steel, when she found what she wanted. She picked it up and slipped a wrapper over her shoulders, then softly opened the door of her room to peer out into the hall.

Meanwhile as to the Seven whom we left standing inside of the window down near the other end. They were, as has been said, entirely unconscious of what has just been mentioned. Texas had crept forward and extinguished the light that burned in the hall, and they were now standing in total darkness but for the single ray of the lantern. They held a whispered conversation as to what they should do next.

Parson Stanard volunteered to pick the lock of Chandler's door; he wasn't a burglar by profession, by Zeus, said he, but he believed in a gentleman of culture knowing something about all the arts and professions. (This was whispered in all seriousness.) And so the Parson crept up to the door, the lantern in his hand. He knelt down before the lock and fell to examining it cautiously, finally thrusting in a bent piece of wire and getting to work. He said he could get that door open in two minutes.

Meanwhile the others were huddled together waiting anxiously. Indian was leaning against the wall, making it shake with his nervous trembling, and Texas was peering out of the window to make sure that there was no sign of danger there. And then suddenly came the thunderclap.

Nothing could be imagined more terrifying to the amateur burglars than what actually happened in the next half minute. There came first the sound of a creaking door, a sound that made them start back. And an instant later a figure sprang out into the hallway, a figure that they could plainly see in the darkness, for it was white as snow. The figure raised one arm and called in a voice that was clear and unfaltering:

"What are you doing there?"

The plebes stood aghast, trembling. They knew the voice, and that but increased their horror. For it was Grace Fuller, their dearest friend!

They all recognized her but one, and that was Texas; Texas had been leaning out of the window and the voice was not so distinct to him. He wheeled about with the swiftness of a panther, giving vent to a cry of anger as he did so. He flung his hand around to his pocket and whipped out his revolver. Before the others could make a move to stop him he swung it up to his shoulder.

And an instant later there came a blinding flash of light and a loud report that awoke the echoes of the silent building.

CHAPTER XII

SEVEN BURGLARS IN A SCRAPE

The scene that followed beggars description. Mark had leaped forward to seize the Texan's hand, shouting aloud:

"Stop! stop! It's Grace Fuller!"

Texas started back in surprise; at the same moment came the shot, which was from the girl's revolver. It was accidental, as she afterward declared, though the plebes did not know it then. The result frightened Grace even more than it did them, the bullet buried itself in the wall, but the sound of the report was followed by a wail of agony from the terrified Indian, which echoed down the hall. And Grace heard shouts from various parts of the hotel, doors opening, people running about, and she knew that her friends were in deadly peril.

A much more hopeless situation it would be hard to imagine; the girl was horrified. But her first thought was had she wounded Indian, and she dashed wildly down the hallway to them.

One glance at the huddled group of figures sufficed to answer that question. Before she could make another sound there came a bounding step upon the stairway.

"We'll be discovered!" cried Mark. "Quick!"

He turned to the window; but a single glance outside showed him two figures running across the lawn. There was no hope of escape there. They were gone!

An instant later Grace Fuller's clear tones rang in his ear.

"Come! Come!"

Like a flash she turned and dashed down the hallway to her room. Mark followed at her heels, and the rest of them, too, dragging the half-paralyzed and terrified Indian along, while the shouts and footsteps swelled louder and louder to urge them on.

They were just in time. Grace Fuller had scarcely time to push the last one in and then slam the door before three men, one of them her father, dashed around a turn of the hall and confronted her white figure standing at the door, the revolver still in her hand.

The huddled plebes inside were too alarmed to think. They heard the quick-witted girl call to the men:

"Here! Hurry up. This way!"

And then they heard the footsteps die away again, as the men with her at their head dashed down the hall toward the rear stairs of the building. They knew that for the time they were safe.

They stood panting and breathless, listening for a moment. They heard the noise at the rear increase; it was evident that everybody was hurrying in that direction. Mark sprang to the window and looked out. He saw three men running toward the foot of the ladder.

"There's where they went up!" he heard one of them say.

And then came a shout from the rear and the three dashed around the building in that direction, leaving the lawn clear and the place deserted. Mark turned and cried to the others:

"Come! Quick! Now's our chance!"

It was a desperate chance, but they took it.

"One dash for the camp," whispered Texas. "Git in an' hide, no matter what!"

They leaped out of the window and made a dash for the ladder. A second or two might make all the difference now. They might get a start, or again they might find a man with a revolver to stop them at the foot. It was a critical situation, and the plebes were quick as lightning, even Indian.

Texas dropped to the ground, and Dewey after him. They could not wait for the others to get down the ladder. Mark slid down like a flash, holding to the side with one hand. Indian slipped halfway and tumbled the rest. Chauncey, Sleepy and the Parson came down one on each side, almost on top of them, and a second or two later the Seven were at the foot staring about them like so many hunted animals.

"Come on!" cried Mark, seeing no one. "For your lives!"

They sprang forward and dashed away toward the camp. They had not gone a dozen yards before there came a shout from the rear of the hotel, a shout that swelled to a roar.

"There they go! Quick! Stop 'em! Halt!"

Halt? Not much! Those plebes were running as never did man

run before. Even Indian was breaking records, fear urging him to prodigies of speed. Fortunately there was no one of the pursuers who was armed, but they were in hot pursuit, and their shouts might have the camp awake any moment.

It was a very short distance to the camp, but to the burglars it seemed a league. They expected a pistol shot any moment, and yet they could not run any faster. They bounded across the path, through the bushes and on, until suddenly a high embankment loomed up before them. It was Fort Clinton, and they dashed around the corner and into the camp beyond.

They were not so quick but that the foremost of those in chase saw clearly where they went; and the cry swelled out upon the breeze:

"The camp! The camp! The burglars are hiding in the camp! Don't let them get out!"

Fortunately the sentry of the post had been at the other end of the path. There was no danger of his recognizing them, but he saw them cross his beat and vanish among the white tents. He heard the cry of "Burglars!" and as he came dashing down the path toward the spot his shouts ran out above the others:

"Corporal of the guard! Post number three!"

Camp McPherson was in an uproar ten seconds after that. The shouting awoke every cadet in the place and brought them all to their tent doors at a bound. The young corporal dashed out of the guard tent and around to the sentry's aid, the tactical officer in command right at his heels with a clank of sword. At the same moment up rushed the crowd of excited half-clad men from the hotel.

"Burglars! Burglars! They're hiding in the camp!"

The lieutenant (the tac) took in the situation in an instant. He dashed down the path, warning the sentries as he ran. The officer at the guard tent turned out the members of the guard a moment later and hurried them away to double the watch about the camp. At the same time the "long roll" was being sounded by a drum orderly up by the color line, summoning the cadets to form at once on the company street.

Truly those burglars were to have a hard time getting out of that trap, into which they had gotten so easily.

Meanwhile, what as to the Banded Seven? The time between when they entered camp and rushed into their two tents and when the company battalion formed was perhaps one minute. In that brief space the plebes had flung off their clothes and hid them feverishly under their blankets, then leaped into their uniforms and fallen into line. And that was the end of their danger.

The battalion once formed there was a hasty roll call, showing all present. And then began a search of the place. The officers, and some of the men from the hotel searched every tent, every spot within the camp. And when they found no burglars they gathered together and stared at each other and wondered how that could be. The tacs interviewed the sentries, and each swore that no burglars or any one else had run across their beats. After which came another search, and another failure, and more mystery.

That those burglars had been cadets on a lark no one dreamed. For they had been desperate-looking burglars, masked and armed. But where were they now?

No one knew, and no one knows to this day. The cadets returned to their tents, discussing the curious situation, and in a few minutes more the camp had settled into its customary stillness.

CHAPTER XIII

WATCHING THE TREASURE

"Any news yet?"

"Nothing. I guess they're waiting till night to move it."

"Do you suppose they knew the burglars were after it last night?"

"No, I don't. They haven't the least idea of it, I'm sure. I heard Bull Harris talking about it this afternoon."

The Seven were waiting for a summons to drill, and sitting in one of the tents of the summer encampment. The cadet who was answering the questions was Mark. He had just entered the tent as the conversation before mentioned began.

"Bull Harris will never get that treasure away from us," he continued. "That is, not unless he has more sense than I think he has. Bull is busy all day, nearly the same as we; so I think he'll try to move it at night. We can watch him then, and stand a fair show to get it back. You see it was only night before last that he stole it from our cave, and I think he's pretty sure we haven't found it out yet. We've been careful not to awaken any suspicions."

"Keerful!" echoed Texas. "Pshaw! I don't see whar the keerful part is. We stole over thar to the hotel last night an' went up to the room and tried to run off with it. An' ef somebody hadn't a seen us, we'd a had it, too."

"Bull Harris has small idea that those desperate burglars were his old plebe enemies," laughed Mark. "I heard him talking about the burglars to the cadets this morning. He said he thought they had come up from Highland Falls and——"

The conversation was cut short just then by the rattle of a drum, which caused the plebes to spring up and hustle out of the tent in a hurry to "fall in" for the morning drill in evolutions, which ended the plotting, for that hour at least.

The treasure was still in the hotel. By way of penance for her last night's stupidity, Grace Fuller had volunteered to see that the chest was not carried from the place that day without the plebes learning of it. Mark had been over to inquire a short while ago; his report had been as stated.

He was mistaken, however, in his idea that the yearling had no idea who the burglars were. Young Chandler had picked up a revolver dropped in the hall by Texas. Texas hadn't missed it; he had too many for that. But this one had his initials on it, and Chandler had "caught on" to the state of affairs in no time. So Bull did know that he was watched, and he was using all his cunning to outwit his unsuspecting enemies. A chest of gold was a stake worth playing hard for.

Slowly the day passed. Chandler still held on to that revolver, with the "J. P." on the hilt. Likewise to the box of treasure in the corner of his room. And he and Bull were busily plotting a way to remove it to safety, and if possible get its real owners into trouble besides. Bull thought they might make another effort to steal it. "It would be just like the fools," said he, "and if they do, they won't get away quite so easily again."

Bull had a decided advantage in the matter, as you may easily see. He was working with his eyes open. He knew the situation. The Seven, on the other hand, were blinded by their supposition that they were unwatched and unsuspected.

Moreover, Bull had what Texas would have called the "drop" on them with that gun.

He was going to cap the climax by getting the treasure safely out of reach; then he calculated that his long-sought revenge over Mark would be obtained.

Bull watched Mark and his "gang" slyly during the day. Bull hated each and every individual member of that gang with all the concentrated hatred of which he was capable. Mark had foiled and outwitted him at every turn—the wild and woolly Texan had thrashed him once; "Indian," the fat and timid "kid" from Indianapolis, had gotten mad one day and interrupted one of Bull's hazing bees, attacking the yearling with a fury that had knocked him off his feet.

Then there was the Parson, who was one of the most inoffensive scholars this world has ever made, but he did object to being tied in a sack "like a member of the Turkish harem," as he vividly described it. And when Bull tried that, the Parson had a fit and put his classical and geological muscles at work on Bull's nose.

Then came "B'gee" Dewey, light-hearted, with a laugh that put everybody in a good humor. Not so Bull; Dewey had once had the nerve to refuse to climb a tree because Bull said to, and had given Bull two black eyes during the scrimmage that followed. Besides these there were "Chauncey, the dude," and "Sleepy, the farmer," who had once attacked Bull and five other yearlings, and who, besides this, had dared to join Mallory's gang, an unpardonable offense anyhow. Bull Harris had much to revenge, but he thought he was about to make up for all of it in a very brief time.

The day passed without incident to interest us. It was the usual routine of duty for the plebes, with much drilling and very little rest. Grace Fuller kept some one watching Chandler all day with no result; and that is all there is to be said.

The plot began to unfold itself that night, however. Chandler strolled in to see Bull after supper, a fact which the Seven noticed with no small amount of glee.

"He's fixing up something for to-night," they whispered.

That seemed to be the state of affairs for a fact, and the Seven made a compact then and there to stay awake and prevent it if it was the last thing they ever did in their lives.

That is, all of them but one. The one was the Parson. The Parson, it appeared, had been "geologizing" during the morning; he had secured some extraordinary specimens of rocks. There were pyrites and fluorites, belemnites and ammonites, hematites, andalusies and goniatites, to say nothing of Hittites and Jebusites, added by the facetious Dewey, with outasites and gottabites. However that may be, Parson Stanard had found a piece of "horn-blend, with traces of potassium nitrate manifested." So extraordinary a phenomenon as that could not be allowed to pass unnoticed, especially for any quantity of ordinary twenty-two carat gold, with no interest to the chemist whatsoever. The Parson vowed he was going to analyze that specimen that evening as soon as camp was quiet.

Dewey suggested that evening ought to be pretty good time to test for "nitrates," whereupon the Parson turned away with a solemn look of pain and fell to examining his chemicals. The Parson had discovered a loose board in the flooring of his tent, and with true Bostonian originality he had hidden all his specimens and apparatus under that; the Texan's revolvers were there, too, making a most interesting collection of articles altogether.

We must go on to the adventures of the evening. The Parson's chemistry was destined to play a most important part in the affair, but not just at present.

Tattoo sounded, calling the cadets to roll call and bed; taps comes half an hour later, "lights out and all quiet." Then the "tac" inspected and went to bed also, after which the Parson got up, let down his tent walls, lighted his candle, and set out his array of test-tubes and reagents. Then also Texas got up and stole out of the tent, past the sentry, and over to the hotel.

It had been agreed that the place was to be watched from the distance every moment that night. Texas had put in a claim to be first, and he was on his way to spend an hour hiding in the bushes. Chandler and Bull Harris weren't going to remove that treasure without a "scrap."

As it happened, Texas was not going to have to wait long. It appears that Bull imagined that the Seven were going to try burglary again; his plan to fool them was to hide the treasure early, before the people in the hotel were quiet, and so before the plebes could do anything. Then, the treasure once out of the way, Chandler might easily trap the plebes. It was quite a clever scheme indeed, and Bull was in a hurry to put it into execution.

He stole out of camp as Texas had done, and stole into the hotel at the rear entrance. At the same moment Texas rose up out of the bushes and sped away toward camp at the top of his speed.

Which was where the excitement began.

CHAPTER XIV

THE SEVEN IN A TRAP

Some ten minutes after Bull Harris vanished in the shadow of the hotel, two figures came down the stairs, bearing a heavy burden between them. There was no one in the neighborhood to observe them. They crept out the back door and gently deposited their load upon a wheelbarrow that stood near. A moment more and they and the wheelbarrow, too, had disappeared in the shadow of the trees.

At the same instant six figures dashed past the sentry at the camp and set out to follow swiftly. They were the members of the Banded Seven, minus the chemical Parson. The other two were Chandler and his cousin.

The latter were wary as foxes; they were aware of the fact that they might be followed, and Bull was glancing over his shoulder at every step. But owing to the sentries that patrol the post, he had to keep in the dark shadow of the woods by the river front, and that was where the six got their chance to hide. They were cautious, too; even our fat friend, Joseph Smith, was as silent and stealthy as any genuine "Indian."

Bull and his companion skirted the buildings to the south, and emerged upon the road to Highland Falls. Down this they hurried for a short distance, and then turned into a patch of thick woods just above cadet limits. In the center of the woods they halted, set down their load and went right to work without further parley. They were going to bury the treasure, where it would be safe beyond possibility of danger.

That was their plan. To be very brief, I may say that they did not get far. Bull had barely had time to plunge his spade into the ground before there came a sound of a snapping twig that made him start as if he had been shot.

It was a dark night, very dark, and the two frightened rascals could distinguish little. But one thing they did see; that was the grinning countenance of the "son o' the Hon. Scrap Powers, o'

Hurricane County, Texas," at the present moment peering over the barrel of a luminous and voluminous revolver.

There never was a hold up more sudden and complete than that, at least not in the experience of our cowboy friend. Chandler had a revolver in his pocket (the one that Texas had dropped), but he did not dare to make a move to touch it. He was too well aware of Jeremiah Powers' reputation among the cadets. Chandler and Bull could do nothing but stare and gasp.

It was not part of the programme of the six to keep them in suspense for any time. Texas kept his gun leveled, reinforced by another in his other hand, while Mark and his companions, smiling cheerfully, stepped out and proceeded to take possession in genuine Dick Turpin style.

In the first place, there were the prisoners to be attended to. They were too much confounded and frightened to resist, and they speedily found themselves lying flat as pancakes on the ground, tied hand and foot, with handkerchiefs in their mouths for an extra precaution. Then, and then only, Texas shoved his revolvers back where they came from; and the others laid hold of the wheelbarrow and the whole crowd strolled merrily away, whistling meanwhile.

For which please score one for the Banded Seven.

Unfortunately, their triumph was destined to be a very transitory one. I blush to record it of my most cautious and wary friend from Texas, but it is true, and truth must be told. Texas actually forgot to search his man when he held him up! The result was that the revolver, a terrible bit of evidence, was still in Chandler's pocket. But that was not all. So sure were the six plebes of their complete triumph, that they even failed to tie their prisoners apart.

The last of the party had scarcely turned away before Bull, glancing about him with his cunning, catlike eyes, rolled swiftly over until he was at his cousin's side. He bit at the rope that tied the latter's hands; he could not have chewed more savagely if he had hold of Mallory's flesh. Chandler's hands were free in a moment, and it was the work of but a few moments more to whip out his knife and loosen Bull. The sound of the plebes' merry laughter had not died away in the woods before the two were on the trail, creeping stealthily up behind their unsuspecting victims with their load of gold. And Chandler had the revolver in his hand now by way of a precaution.

Not so very far back in the woods on the way to Highland Falls stood an old and dilapidated icehouse. Some may remember that icehouse; it figured rather prominently in one of Mark's adventures. Mark had not been in West Point a week before his cheerful friend Bull had tried to lock him up in that place so as to have him absent from réveille. Bull had failed, fortunately, and Mark had turned the tables on him. Bull had had unpleasant recollections of that icehouse ever since.

It was toward that building the six happy and triumphant plebes were heading; Mark had chanced to think of it, and of the fact that its soft sawdust would make a most excellent hiding place for the wonderful treasure. The plebes could hardly realize that they had that treasure safe. After all the vicissitudes it had been through, all the disappointments and anxiety it had caused them, it seemed to be too good to be true. And they ran their fingers through the chinking contents of the old chest; it was too dark to see it, but they could feel it, and that was enough to make them chuckle for joy.

They were in a particularly jolly humor as they hurried through the woods. Dewey was as lively as a kitten, and was being reminded of jokes enough to take up the rest of this story; and he kept it up until the building they were looking for loomed up in front of them.

The plebes lost no time about the matter; they opened the creaky door and the whole six of them hurried in to superintend the all-important burial ceremony.

Their figures had scarcely been lost in the darkness before the other two stole out of the woods and halted at the edge of the clearing. The two were stooping low, creeping with the stealth of catamounts. So silent were they there was not even the snap of a twig to betray them, and when they stopped they scarcely dared breathe as they listened. One of the crouching figures clutched a revolver in his hand; the other's fists were clinched until the nails dug into his flesh. His teeth were set, and his eye gleamed with a hatred and resentment that he alone knew how to feel. Bull Harris felt that his time had come, the time he had waited for, for two long months of concentrated yearning.

There were sounds of muffled laughter from inside, and the thud of the spade that some one was using. Bull glanced at his companion.

"Are you ready?" he whispered.

And the other nodded, though his hand shook.

"Are you afraid?" hissed Bull. "It is a risk, for that fiend of a Texan may fight. You may have to shoot. Do you hear me?"

Once more Chandler nodded, and gripped the revolver like a vise.

There was not another word said. The two crouched low and stepped out of the shadow of the bushes. Silently as the shadows themselves they sped across the open space. And then suddenly Bull halted again; for the sound of murmuring voices from inside the little building grew audible as they advanced.

"B'gee, it's a regular Captain Kidd business! I don't think Bull was a success as a Kidd, that is, if you spell it with two d's. He——"

"Say, Mark," interrupted another voice, "do you remember the time that ole coyote tried to lock you in hyar? Doggone his boots, I bet he don't try that very soon again."

"I'm afraid not," laughed Mark, softly. "Bull had his chance once, but he failed to make the most of it."

And at the words Bull seized his cousin convulsively by the arm and forced him back. Before the other could see what the yearling meant he had sprung forward, gasping with rage. The next instant the heavy door creaked and swung too.

Mark and his allies started back in alarm. Before they could make another move, before they could even think, they heard the rusty lock grate, heard a heavy log jammed against the door to hold it tight.

And then a low, mocking laugh of triumph rang on their ears. Bull Harris' time had come at last.

CHAPTER XV

BUYING THEIR RELEASE

Our business just now is with Parson Stanard, the scholarly geologist and chemist, sitting all by himself in his silent tent and diligently analyzing his hematites and gottabites and outasights. The Parson made a curious figure; you would have laughed if you could have seen him. A solitary candle gave the flickering light by which he worked.

The Parson was a trifle agitated about that candle, because, as you know, it is the correct thing for a scholar to burn "midnight oil." The midnight part was all right, but it took a long stretch of the imagination to convert tallow into kerosene. That kind of chemistry was too much for even the Parson.

However, it had to be borne. The Parson was seated in tailor fashion, in spite of which posture he was managing as usual to display his sea-green socks to the light. He had a row of bottles in a semicircle about him, like so many soldiers on parade; and at that moment he was engaged in examining a most interesting and complicated filtrate.

Parson Stanard was at the climax of his important night's work. It will be remembered he was testing for potassium nitrate. He had it. He had put some of the substance in the fire and gotten the violet flame he wanted. Then, to make sure, he reached forward and took one of the bottles.

But the Parson never made that test. If the Banded Seven had seen him at that moment they would assuredly have been frightened, for his face underwent a most startling and amazing transformation. He had picked up the bottle; glanced at its label. And the next instant his eyes seemed fairly to pop up out of his head. His jaw dropped, his hands relaxed, and the wondrous and long-sought powder was scattered over the floor.

The Parson was ordinarily a quick thinker, but it took a time for that thought, whatever it was, with all its horrible import, to flash across his mind. And meanwhile his face was a picture of consternation.

Then suddenly he leaped to his feet with a perfect gasp of horror, knocking the candle over and making the bottles rattle.

"By the thunderbolts of Jove!" he cried. "By the hounds of Diana! By the distaff of Minerva!"

The Parson was striding up and down his tent by this time, utterly regardless of chemistry, geology, and possible discovery in the bargain.

"By the steeds of Apollo!" he muttered. "By the waters of the Styx, by the scepter of Zeus, by the cap of Mercury, by the apple of Venus and the bow of Ulyssus! By the nine immortals and the Seven Hills of Rome!——"

At this stage of the proceedings the agitated chemist was out in the company street, and striding away in the darkness.

"By the eagle of Ganymede, by the shield of Mars, by the temple of Janus, by the trident of Neptune!"

During this the gentleman was speeding out of camp, causing the sentry, who thought he was crazy, so much alarm that he forgot to challenge. By the time he recovered the Parson was gone and only an echo of his voice remained——

"By the forge of Vulcan, by the cave of Æolus, by the flames of Vesta!"

Not to continue the catalogue, which it would be found contained all the mythology from Greek and Sanskrit to Hindoostanee, suffice it to say that the agitated scholar strode straight down the road to Highland Falls with all the speed that a scholar could assume without loss of dignity and breath. Also that he turned off the road at the precise place his comrades had and vanished in the woods.

"They said they were going to bury it in the icehouse," muttered the Parson. "It is there I shall endeavor to intercept them and inform them of this most extraordinary conditions of affairs. Yea, by the all-wise, high-thundering Olympian Zeus."

The more excited the Parson got the more Homeric epithets it was his custom to heap upon the helpless head of his favorite divinity; he was very much excited just now.

Fortunately, the Parson did not know just where the icehouse was; he had never been to it but once, and he wandered about the woods hunting in vain for at least half an hour. Then he sat down in despair and gasped for breath, and listened. And in that way he was suddenly made aware of the whereabouts of the object of his search.

A sound came to his ears, a loud laugh in the distance.

"Ho, ho! You fools! Dig a tunnel, hey? Ho, ha! Well, suppose you dig it. I've a revolver here, and I'll blow the blamed head off the first man that comes out. How do you like that. Guess again, Mark Mallory."

The Parson sprang up as if he had sat down on the proverbial haystack with a needle in it. That voice was the voice of the "enemy," Bull Harris! A moment later the Parson was creeping toward the sound with stealthiness that would have done credit to an Apache.

"We are in the hands of the enemy," he gasped. "By the all-wise, high-thundering, far-ruling Olympian Zeus!"

"Ho, ho!" roared the voice, nearer now. "Think you can break the door down, hey? Well! well! Guess I'll have to put a new log against it. How do you like that! That's right! Whack away! Bully! Keep it up and you may get out by to-morrow night. Ho! ho!"

The unfortunate Zeus got a few more epithets then, and the Parson crept nearer still. In fact, he got so near that peering out of the bushes, he could spy the clearing with the little building and the two figures dancing gayly in front of it. Bull Harris was fairly convulsed with joy.

"I've got my revenge!" he roared. "I've got it! I told you I'd get it! Didn't I tell you so? I told you I'd have you B. J. plebes out of here if I died for it. And now my time's come! Hooray! You'll be found to-morrow, beyond cadet limits, and out you go. You can't deny it! How do you like it?"

"You'll go to Halifax! you ole coyote," growled a smothered voice from the inside.

"Me! Ho, ho! What do I care? I've nothing to lose. I'm ready to go. But you—ho, ho! Ask that fool Mallory how he likes it."

"Very well," responded a cheery voice. "You must remember that we've got the treasure."

"Much good it'll do you," chuckled Bull. "You'll be in State's prison in a week or so. Ho, ho! Let's tell 'em, Chandler. The secret's too good a one to keep. Ask Texas what became of the revolver he dropped in the hotel last night playing burglar. The revolver with the initials J. P. on it."

That was a thunderbolt. From the way it struck the horrified prisoners dumb. Bull knew it, and laughed with yet more malignant glee.

"You can't prove it!" roared Texas furiously.

"Can't I?" chuckled Bull. "You'd hate to have me try. It would take all your gold to get you out of that scrape, I fancy. Ho, ho! Court-martial! State's prison! I guess I've got the best of it for once."

"It's the first time," growled Texas.

During all this the Parson had been hiding in the bushes, trembling, gasping, slowly taking in the situation, the dilemma his friends were in. All thoughts of the excitement under which he had originally set out were gone. He was cudgeling his head to see what he was to do to turn the tide of battle.

It was a difficult problem, for Chandler had a revolver and the Parson had none. This was evidently a case where cunning and not brute force were to tell, and the Parson knitted his learned brows thoughtfully. Meanwhile the conversation was going on, and taking a new turn. Bull Harris had a proposition.

"I suppose you fellows are ready to acknowledge you're beaten," he sneered. "And I suppose you've got sense enough to see what a fix you're in."

To tell the truth, the whole Seven saw it clearly, but they were not ready to acknowledge it to Bull.

"I just want to say," the latter continued, after a moment's pause, "that there's a way for you fools to get out of this. If you don't choose to do it you may as well make up your minds to stay all night."

"I suppose," responded Mark, laughing at this introduction to a very obvious offer. "I suppose you think we're going to let you get hold of our treasure. I suppose you think we'll purchase our freedom with that."

"That's what I do," said Bull, "else you stay."

"We'll stay," laughed Mark, coolly. "And you can go to blazes."

This proposition was not lost upon the Parson, lying in the bushes outside. The Parson had drunk in every word of it, and for some reason began to gasp and wriggle with suppressed excitement as he realized the meaning of the offer. As Mark spoke the last time the Parson slid back into the woods and stole softly around to the rear of the little building.

A few moments later, Mark, to his astonishment, heard a faint whisper in one of the crevices at the back. "Say, Mark!" That voice Mark would have known had he heard it in China. He ran to the spot and there was a minute's quick conversation. At the end of it the Parson turned and crept way again, unseen by the two in front.

Perhaps five minutes later Bull Harris, who was still crowing merrily, was electrified to learn that the plebes had reconsidered their first defiance—that the gold was his!

"I guess we'll have to give it up," said Mark, briefly. "You've got us, and that's all that there is to it."

"Do you mean," cried Bull, unable to hide his joy, "that if we let you out and give you the revolver you are willing to give up the treasure altogether?"

"Yes," said Mark. "We are."

"But how am I trust you?" demanded Bull. "If I open the door how do I know you won't——"

"I've said I wont!" interrupted Mark, with angry emphasis. "You know me, I guess."

It was a funny thing. Bull himself would have lied all day without his conscience troubling him. But somehow or other he was sure that Mark wouldn't. In spite of his cousin's protestations, he stepped forward, removed the barricades and turned the key.

The six plebes came out, looking sheepish enough. Texas received his lost revolver meekly, though he felt like braining Bull with it. A minute later the six hurried off into the woods, leaving

Bull and his cousin to gloat for hours over the chest of gold they left inside.

Truly, it was a triumph for Bull.

CHAPTER XVI

BULL HARRIS REAPS HIS REWARD

It was the evening of the following day, and the scene was Highland Falls. It was about twelve o'clock at night, to be more exact as to time; as to place, the scene was a low tavern on the roadside.

This hour was long after the time that cadets are supposed to be in their tents asleep, but as we have seen, cadets do not always do as they are supposed to. It is safe to say that in spite of all the talk about the severity of West Point discipline, if the commandant of cadets should take it into his head to wander through Camp McPherson every night for a week running, he would find some things to surprise him. He might not find any geological chemists hard at work, but he might find a small game of some sort going on on the sly, and he'd be sure to find a surreptitious banquet or two. He might also see occasional parties steal past an obliging sentry who was looking the other way. It is probable, however, that none of this would surprise him very much, for he did it all himself in his day.

There are always bolder and more reckless spirits who are ever ready for such a lark, enjoying it in proportion to the risk they run. There are always some among these who think it manly to drink and smoke, and frequent low places; it is upon one of these latter assemblages that we are about to look in. We must not mind a rather unpleasant odor of bad tobacco, or a still more unpleasant odor of bad liquor.

It is quite needless to say that one of the crowd was Bull Harris; it would be hard to find a crowd of cadets amusing themselves as these were without Bull among them. This tavern was the regular resort of him and his "gang" on occasions when they visited Highland Falls. It has not been mentioned before, because the less said about such places the better.

Bull liked this place for many reasons. It was quiet, and there was nobody to disturb them. Then, too, the proprietor, a fat

Irishman, known as "Jake," was a man who told no secrets and minded his own business, thus keeping an ideal place for a crowd of young "gentlemen" to come for a lark. Bull was there to-night, and what was more important, he was acting as host. Bull was "blowing off" his friends.

There was first, his Cousin Chandler, whom we know; then there was Gus Murray, who needs but little introduction. As an ally and worshiper of Bull and a malignant enemy of Mark Mallory's, Gus Murray yielded to no one, with the possible exception of Merry Vance, the shallow and sour-faced youth on his right. The cause of Merry's pessimistic complexion we once guessed to be indigestion; inasmuch as he was just then pouring down his third dose of bad brandy a revision of this surmise will be allowed. To complete the party, there was one more, a very small one, our young friend, Baby Edwards, a sweet-tempered little sneak who had not even manliness enough to be vicious.

When we peered in the party was in full swing. Baby Edwards had half gone to sleep, having drunk two glasses of beer. Bull had just completed for the third time a graphic description of how that Mallory had been duped, a story which was a never-failing source of interest and hilarity to the rest, who were whacking their glasses on the table and cheering merrily, in fact, so merrily that the cautious proprietor was forced to come to the door and protest.

"How much did you say it was worth?" demanded Vance, after the man had gone away again.

"Fifty thousand dollars," chuckled Bull. "Fifty thousand if a cent. Fill 'em up, boys. Chandler and I calculated it weighed two hundred pounds. Whoop!"

Merry's eyes glistened feverishly as he listened, whether from brandy or from what he heard it would be hard to say.

"Whereabouts is it now?" demanded he. "Are you sure Mallory can't get it?"

"Dead sure," laughed Bull. "Do you suppose I'd be fool enough to let Mallory sneak up behind me twice. Not much! It's safe."

"Whereabouts?"

"Oh, it's buried up here in the woods a piece," said the other, cautiously. "It's where we can get it any time we want to. Oh, say, but it's fine to know you're rich—no trouble about paying any confounded bills. And that Irish villain Jake can't kick because we drink more than we can pay for. Whoop! Help yourselves!"

The others were helping themselves for all they were worth. It seldom happened to that crowd to get a chance such as this, and cadet duties might go to blazes in the meantime. They were singing and shouting and fast getting themselves into a very delightful state, indeed, keenly enjoying themselves every minute of the time, so they thought.

Fun like that can't last very long, however. Baby Edwards went to sleep as I said! it is to be hoped he dreamed of better things. Merry Vance got quiet and stupid also, while Gus Murray waxed cross and ugly. So pretty soon Bull concluded it was time to go home. Anybody who glanced at the bottles scattered about on the floor and table would have thought so too.

At this stage of the game Jake bowed himself in. Jake was usually a Nemesis, an undesired person altogether, for he came to collect. But Bull didn't mind this time.

"I wants me money," began the man, surlily, gazing about him at the scene of destruction. "An' what's more, I wants to say you fellows has got to make less noise here nights. I ain't goin' to have my license taken away for no cadet. See?"

Bull gazed at him sneeringly during this discourse.

"Anything more?" he demanded.

"Yes, there is. You fellers ain't a-comin' here no more till you pays yer bills. This is the third time you've tried to let 'em run, an' by thunder I ain't a-goin' to stand it. I don't believe you've got no money anyhow, an' I'm goin' to stop this——"

"Oh, shut up, confound ye!" broke in Bull, impatiently. "Who asked you to trust them? Don't be a fool! Take that and shut up your mouth."

These not over polite remarks came as Bull flung three or four of the five-dollar gold pieces with a lordly air onto the table. The fellow eyed them greedily, then gathered them up and left the room.

Bull turned to rouse his companions, chuckling to himself as he did so.

"Come on, boys," said he. "Get up there and hustle."

Baby Edwards, having been kicked unceremoniously to the floor, got up growling. Merry Vance likewise wanted to fight Gus, who woke him. But the five got started finally and made for the door. Beyond that, however, they did not get, for there they encountered the brawny form of Jake.

"Stop!" said he, briefly.

"What do you want now?" demanded Bull.

The other extended his hand, in which lay the coins.

"Don't want 'em," said he.

Bull stared at him in amazement.

"Don't want 'em!" he echoed. "In the name of Heaven why not?"

"No good," said the other, sententiously.

The effect of those two words upon Bull was like that of a bullet; he staggered back against the wall, gasping, his eyes fairly starting out of his head. The others understood dimly and turned pale.

It took several minutes for that idea to dawn upon Bull Harris in all its frightful horror. When he realized it he sprang forward with a shriek.

"No good!" he cried. "Great Heavens, man, what do you mean?"

The proprietor's response was brief, but effective. He put his hand in his pocket and brought out a shining stone. He rubbed it against the gold and held it up so that Bull might see the color that resulted.

"'Tain't gold," said he. "It's counterfeit."

Bull staggered back against the wall again. Counterfeit! Counterfeit! He saw it all now! Saw why Mallory had given it up! Saw what a fool he—Bull Harris—had been! Saw that he had let them out of the trap, given them the weapon, the only proof. Let them go in safety, leaving him a chest full of brass. It made Bull sick to think of it. Oh, surely it could not be true!

Another thought flashed over him then. Why had Mallory

fought so for it, why been so reluctant to give it up? No, it must be genuine! It must be a mistake! Perhaps those few were bad, but all the coins could not be. Trembling with dread, Bull sprang forward, wrenched the stone from the hand of the astonished "Jake," burst out of the place, and sped away up the road.

The man was at his heels at this effort to dodge him without paying. Behind him rushed the other four, frightened and sobered by this terrible blow. But Bull's anxiety lent speed to him and he easily outdistanced the crowd.

When they came upon him again they found him in the woods on his knees, digging savagely in the ground with his fingers. In response to his shouts they flung themselves down to help him, while the breathless Irishman stood by and stared in amazement.

Bull was in a frenzy. He fairly tore his way down to the chest, and seizing it by the handles, jerked it out with the strength of a Hercules. He flung back the lid, jerked the bit of rock from his pocket, and seized a handful of the coins.

A moment more and he staggered back, and sank to the ground, limp and helpless.

The chest of "gold" was worthless.

We must revert to the conversation of the Seven the night before, for the benefit of those who are curious. Mark and his friends, as they disappeared in the woods, were joined by the solemn Parson. You may believe that it was a merry crowd.

"Look here, Parson," demanded Mark, the first thing. "Are you sure that money is no good?"

"Sure?" echoed the Parson. "Sure as I am that the most reliable and mathematical of all the sciences is true. Perhaps you will wish, gentlemen, that I explain to you the most extraordinary state of affairs. I shall do so, yea, by Zeus. I feel that I owe it to myself by way of explanation of a most unaccountable—ahem—blunder I have made."

The Parson drew a long breath and continued.

"Gentlemen," said he, "when first we set out upon that treasure hunt I took with me two bottles of acid. One was a test for the presence of argenic compounds, that is, silver, and the other for what is popularly designated gold. In the excitement of the discovery of the chest, to my everlasting humiliation, be it said, I used the wrong acid. The reaction I got proved the presence of copper. I thought it was gold."

After this extraordinary speech of self-abnegation the Parson bowed his head in shame. It was at least a minute before he could muster the courage to go on. Truly that had been a frightful blunder for an analytical chemist to make.

"To-night," he continued at last, "I was testing for potassium, and I reached for that bottle of gold reagent. I expected to find it half empty. I found it full, and I knew in an instant that I could not have used a drop of it. Gentlemen, that told me the story of my error. I shall do penance for it as long as I may live."

CHAPTER XVII

THE SEVEN MAKE A NEW MOVE

"For Heaven's sake, man, what has happened?"

The cause of this exclamation was Dewey. At the moment his uniform was dirty and torn, and his face was far from handsome. It was bruised and blue in lumps, and there were ugly places of a bright red, lending a startling effect indeed.

The speaker was Mark. He had been sitting at his tent door rubbing his gun diligently, but he sprang up in alarm when he espied the other.

"What on earth has happened to you, Dewey?" he repeated.

Dewey laughed to himself, in spite of his sorry condition.

"I don't exactly know," he said. "B'gee, I've forgotten lots of things in the last ten minutes. I'll come in and think 'em over and tell you."

He entered the tent, and after gazing at himself ruefully in the looking-glass that hung by the tent pole, wet a towel and fell to washing things gently.

"B'gee!" he muttered, "Mark Mallory, there's going to be no end of trouble on account of this."

"You haven't told me yet," said the other. "You don't mean that you've been getting hazed some more?"

"Would you call it hazing," responded Dewey, "if you'd been pummeled until you looked like rare beef? You needn't be getting angry about it. We'll have plenty of time for that later. Meantime, just you listen to my tale of woe, b'gee! I was down on Flirtation Walk a while ago, off in a lonely part. And all of a sudden I came across half a dozen yearlings. One of them was Bull Harris, and when he saw me he turned to the other cadets and called: 'There's one of the gang now! We might just as well start at what we agreed on.' And then, b'gee, they started. Do you think that eye'll shut up entirely?"

"What did they do?" demanded Mark, his blood boiling as he surveyed his comrade's bruises.

"Well, b'gee, they sailed up, in the first place, and began a lot of talking. 'You belong to that Mallory gang, don't you?' said Bull Harris. 'Yes,' says I, 'I do, and I'm proud of it, too. What's the matter with Mallory?' 'Matter?' roared Gus Murray. 'B'gee, he's the confoundedest freshest plebe that ever came to this academy. Hasn't he dared to refuse to let us haze him? Hasn't he played all kinds of tricks upon us, made life miserable for us? Hasn't he even dared to go to the hop, something no plebe has ever dared to do in the history of West Point?' 'Seeing that you're asking the question, b'gee,' I said, 'I don't mind telling you by way of answer that he has, and also that he's outwitted you and licked you at every turn. And that he'll do it again the first chance he gets, and b'gee, I'll be there to help him, too! How's that?'"

Here the reckless youngster paused while he removed the cork of a vaseline bottle; then he continued:

"That made old Bull wild; he hates you like fury, Mark, and he's simply wild about the way we fooled him with that treasure. He began to rear around like a wild man. 'If you fool plebes think we're going to stand your impudence,' he yelled, 'you're mistaken! I want you to understand that we've found out about that confounded organization Mallory's gotten up among the plebes to fight us——'"

"Did he say that?" cried Mark, in surprise. "How did they learn?"

"They didn't," said Dewey. "They don't know we call it the Banded Seven, or anything else about it, but they've seen us together so much when they've tried to haze us that they've sort of guessed it. Anyway, they've determined to break it up, b'gee."

"They have! How?"

"Simply by walloping every man in it, b'gee. And they started on yours truly. The whole crowd piled on at once, Mark."

"The cowards!" exclaimed Mark.

"Well, I gave 'em a good time, anyway," laughed Dewey, whose natural light-heartedness had not been marred in the least. "I made for Bull. B'gee, I was bound one of them would be sorry, and I chose him. I lammed him two beauties and tumbled him into a ditch. But by that time they had me down. And——"

"Where are the rest of the Seven?" cried Mark, springing up impatiently. "By George, I'm going to get square for this outrage if it's the last thing I ever do in my life. I'll fight them fair just as long as they want it. I'm ready to meet any man they send, as I did. But, by jingo, I won't stand the tricks of that miserable coward Bull Harris another day. He's done nothing but try to get me into scrapes since the day I came here, and refused to let him haze me. And now I'm going to stop it or bust. Where are the rest of the fellows?"

"I don't know," began Dewey, but he was interrupted by an answer from an unexpected quarter. Texas came rushing down the company street and bounded into Mark's tent.

He, too, was marred with the scars of battle. His clothing was soiled, and his bronzed features were sadly awry. And Texas was wild.

"Wow!" he roared, his words fairly tripping each other up, in such rapid succession did they come. "Whoop! Say, you fellows, you dunno what you been a-missin'! I ain't had so much fun since the day I come hyar. Jes' had the rousin'est ole scrap I ever see. There was a dozen of 'em, them ole yearlin's, and they all piled on to once. Whoop! Mark, git up thar an' come out an' help me finish it."

Texas was prancing around the tent in excitement, his fingers twitching furiously. He gasped for breath for a moment, and then continued.

"It was that air ole Bull Harris and his gang. Bull had been a-fightin' somebody else, cuz one eye was black."

"Bully, b'gee!" put in Dewey.

"An' he was mad's a hornet. 'Look a yere,' says he, 'you rarin' ole hyena of a cowboy, I want you to understand that you an' that air scoundrel Mallory' — — an', Mark, I never gave him a chance for another word, jes' piled right in. An' then all the rest of 'em lit on to me an' there was the wust mess I ever heerd tell of."

Angry though Mark was, he could not help being amused at the hilarity of his bloodthirsty friend and fellow-warrior, who was still dancing excitedly about the tent.

"Who won?" inquired Mark.

"I dunno," said Texas. "I never had a chance to find out. First they jumped on me and smothered me, an' then I got out and jumped on them, only there was so many I couldn't sit on 'em all to once, an' so I had to git up ag'in. Oh, say, 'twas great. I wish some o' the boys could a' been thar to see that air rumpus. An' I ain't through yit, either. I'm a-goin' to lambast them air yearlin's—what d'ye say, Mark?"

Texas gazed at his friend inquiringly; and Mark gripped him by the hand.

"I'll help you," he said. "I'm going to settle that crowd for once and for all if I have to put them in hospital. And now let's go out and hunt for the rest of the Seven and see what's happened to them."

Mark's patience was about exhausted; he had stood much from Bull Harris, but as he left that tent and strode out of camp with the other two at his side, there was a set look about his mouth and a gleam in his eyes that meant business.

He had scarcely crossed the color line that marked the western edge of the camp before he caught sight of one more of the Seven. And Mark had seen him but an instant before the thought flashed over him that this one had been through just the same experience as Texas and "B'gee" Dewey.

The new arrival was Parson Stanard. His face was not scarred, but it was red with anger, and his collar was wilted by excitement which betrayed itself even in his hasty stride as he walked.

"Yea, by Zeus!" he cried, as soon as he reached his friends. "Gentlemen, I have tidings. The enemy is risen! Even now he is hot upon our trail. My spirit burns within me like that of Paul Revere, the messenger of liberty, riding forth from good old Boston town. Boston, cradle of liberty, father of— —"

The Parson's news was exciting, but even then he could not withstand the temptation to deliver a discourse upon the merits of his native town. Mark had to set him straight again.

"Has Bull been after you, too?" he asked.

"Yea!" said the Parson. "He has, and that, too, with exceeding great vehemence. Truly the persistency of the yearling is surprising; like the giant Antaeus of yore, he springeth up afresh for the battle, when one thinks he is subdued at last. Gentlemen, they attacked me absolutely without provocation. I swear it by the undying flame of Vesta. I was peregrinating peacefully when I met them. And without even a word, forsooth, they sprang at me. And mighty was the anger that blazed up in my breast, yea, by Zeus! As Homer, bard immortal of the Hellenic land, sang of the great Achilles, 'his black heart'—er, let me see. By Zeus, how does that line go? It is in the first book, I know, and about the two hundred and seventy-fifth line, but really I——"

"Never mind Homer," laughed Mark. "What about Harris? What did you do?"

"I replied to their onslaughts in the words of Fitz James: 'This rock shall fly from its firm base as soon as I!' The two who reached me first I did prostrate with two concussions that have paralyzed my prehensile apparatus——"

"Bully for the Parson!" roared Texas.

"And then," continued the other sheepishly, "observing, by Zeus, that there were at least a dozen of them, I concluded to think better of my resolution and effect a retreat, remembering the saying that he who runs away may live to renew his efforts upon some more auspicious occasion."

The Parson looked very humble indeed at this last confession; Mark cheered him somewhat by saying it was the most sensible thing he could have done. And Dewey still further warmed his scholarly heart by a distinction that would have done credit to even Lindley Murray, the grammarian.

"You didn't break your resolution," said Dewey.

"Why not?" inquired Stanard.

"Because, b'gee, you vowed you wouldn't fly. And you haven't flown since, that I see. What you did was to flee, b'gee. If you flyed you wouldn't have fleed, but since you fleed you didn't fly. Some day, b'gee, when you've been bitten, you'll understand the difference between a fly and a flea. You'll find that a flea can fly a great deal faster than a fly can flee, b'gee, and that——"

Somebody jumped on Dewey and smothered him again just then, but it wasn't a yearling. He bobbed up serenely a minute later, to find that the Parson's grammatical old ribs had been tickled by the distinction so carefully made.

"People are very grammatical in Boston, aren't they, Parson?" inquired Dewey. "Reminds me of a story I once heard, b'gee—you fellows needn't groan so, because this is the first story I've told to-day. Fellow popped the question to his best girl. She said, 'No, b'gee.' 'Say it again,' says he. 'No!' says she. 'Thanks,' says he. 'Two negatives make an affirmative. You've promised. Where shall we go for our honeymoon?' B'gee, Parson, there's a way for you to fool your best girl. She's sure to say no, and I don't blame her either."

The lively Dewey subsided for a moment after that. But he couldn't keep quiet very long, especially since no one took up the conversation.

"Speaking of oranges," said he, "reminds me of a story I once heard, b'gee——"

"Who was speaking of oranges?" cried Texas.

"I was," said Dewey solemnly, and then fled for his life.

The other three members of the Banded Seven arrived upon the scene just then and put an end to hostilities. Chauncey, Sleepy and Indian had not had the luck to meet with the yearlings yet, and they listened in amazement and indignation while Mark told the story of Bull Harris and his latest tactics.

"Bless my soul," gasped Indian in horror. "I—I'm going home this very day!"

"I'll go home myself," vowed Mark, "if I don't succeed in stopping this sort of business. I honestly think I'd report it to the authorities, only Bull knows I've been out of bounds and he'd tell. As it is, I'm going to settle him some other way, and a way he'll remember, too."

"When?" cried the others.

"This very night."

"And how?"

"The cave!" responded Mark; and it was evident from the way the others jumped at the word that the suggestion took their fancy.

And in half a minute more the Seven had sworn by all the solemn oaths the classic Parson could invent that they would haze Bull Harris and his cronies in "the cave" that night.

CHAPTER XVIII

THE CAPTURE OF MARK

The afternoon of that momentous day passed without incident. Mark noticed Bull Harris glowering at him as he passed his tent, but beyond that the "subduing" programme got no further. The Banded Seven kept near to camp, so as to prevent it.

That is, all of them but one; Sleepy was that one. The lanky farmer was a member of the guard that day, getting his first lessons in the terrible dangers of sentry duty at Camp McPherson. Now it was necessary for some one to go up and fix that cave for the night's work, and since Sleepy succeeded in getting excused during his four hours off duty that afternoon, he was unanimously elected to be the one to attend to the task.

It was to clear away the effects of that treasure hunt that Sleepy went. He removed all traces of the Parson's energetic digging. Also he fixed quite a number of other things, according to Mark's well-planned directions.

"It's evident to me," said Mark, "from the fact that Bull didn't bother me this morning, hating me most, as he does, that he's putting up a plan for to-night."

"He's afraid to tackle you in the day," growled Texas.

"I should say so," chirruped Indian's fat, round voice. "Didn't you lick him once, and the whole crowd besides. Bless my soul!"

"I think," continued Mark, "that we may take it for granted that Bull will try to kidnap me to-night. You know they did that once, took me off into the woods and beat me. They'll beat harder this time. If a big crowd of them tries it you fellows'll just have to make a noise and wake everybody so that they'll have to drop me and run for their tents. But if there's only a few you can follow and overpower them. It all depends."

Texas rubbed his hands gleefully at this attractive programme.

"What are we a-goin' to do when we ketch 'em?" he demanded.

"You leave that to me," laughed Mark, rising from his seat to end the "conference." "I've got a scheme fixed up to frighten them to death. Just wait."

"Just wait" seemed to represent about all there was to do, though the Seven did not like it a bit. They watched dress parade that evening with far less interest than usual, and sighed with relief when the sunset gun finally sounded. It may be interesting to note that there were some other cadets in just exactly the same impatient state of mind.

It was just as Mark had suspected—Bull Harris had a plot.

The sunset gun was welcomed with relief. They spent the evening strolling about the grounds and discussing the effort they were going to make that night, also occasionally chuckling over the "success" of their attacks during the morning. And then tattoo sounded, and they knew that the time was nearer still.

Bull Harris and his three cronies waited until the sentry had called the hour of eleven. They thought the plebes had had time enough to get to sleep then, so they got up and dressed and sallied forth in the darkness. It was cloudy that night, and black, a circumstance which Bull considered particularly fortunate.

There was no hesitation, no delay to discuss what should be done. The four made straight for a certain A company tent; cadets sleep with their tent walls rolled up in hot weather, and so the yearlings could easily see what was inside. They made out three figures stretched out upon the blankets, all sound asleep; the fourth occupant—the farmer—was now diligently marching post.

The four crept up with stealthiness that would have done credit to Indians. A great deal depended on their not awakening Mallory. Bull, who was the biggest and strongest of the crowd, stole into the tent and placed himself at Mallory's feet; Merry Vance and Murray calculated each upon managing one stalwart arm, while to Baby, as smallest, was intrusted the task of preventing outcry from the victim. Having placed themselves, the four precious rascals paused just one moment to gloat over their hated and unsuspecting enemy. And then Bull gave the signal, and as one man they pounced down.

Mallory, awakened out of a sound sleep, found himself as helpless as if he had been buried alive. Bull's sinewy arms were wrapped about his limbs; his hands were crushed to the earth; and Baby was smothering him in a huge towel. They lifted him an instant later and bore him swiftly from the tent.

A whistle was the signal to the sentry, who faced about and let them cross his beat; the four clambered up the embankment and sprang down into Fort Clinton, chuckling to themselves for joy, having secured the hated plebe with perfect success and secrecy. And now he was theirs, theirs to do with as they saw fit. And how they did mean to "soak" him!

All this, of course, was Bull's view of the matter. But there were some things, just a few, that that cunning young gentleman did not know of. The reader will remember that the yearlings had tried that trick on Mark just once before; ever since then Mark's tent was protected by a very simple but effective burglar alarm. There was a thread tied about his foot. That thread the yearlings had not noticed. It broke when they carried off their victim, but it broke because it had tightened about the wrist of Texas, who sat up in alarm an instant later, just in time to observe the four disappearing in the darkness. By the time they had crossed the sentry beat the rest of the Banded Seven were up and dressing gleefully.

After that the result was never in doubt for a moment. The five all crossed the sentry's post without trouble, because they had heard the signal the yearlings gave. And a moment later the triumphant kidnapers, who were off in a lonely corner of the deserted fort binding up their prisoner as if he were a mummy, were horrified to find themselves confronted by five stalwart plebes.

Bull and his gang were helpless. They did not dare make any outcry, in the first place, because they were more to blame than the plebes in case of discovery, and in the second, because they were "scared to death" of that wild cowboy, who had already made his name dreaded by riding out and holding up the whole artillery squadron. But, oh, how they did fairly grit their teeth in rage!

The imperturbable Texas stood and faced them, twirling two revolvers carelessly while they had the unspeakable humiliation of watching the others ungaging and unbinding the delighted

Mallory, who rose to his feet a moment later, stretched his arms and then merrily took command.

Bull Harris was selected, as leader and head conspirator, to undergo the first torture. Mark placed himself in front of him, and with a light smile upon his face.

"Lie down!" said he.

Bull found himself staring into the muzzle of one of the menacing Texan's revolvers. That took all of Bull's nerve, and he very promptly "lay."

"Now then, Dewey," said Mark, "tie him up."

Dewey used the very ropes that had been meant for Mark. He tied Master Harris' unresisting feet together. Then rolled him unceremoniously over on his back and tied his hands. After which Bull was kicked to one side, and Dewey was ready for the next frightened yet furious victim.

Pretty soon there were four helpless bodies lying side by side within the fort. They were bound hand and foot; there were gags tied in their mouths and heavy towels wrapped about their eyes. And then the Banded Seven were ready.

"Come ahead," said Mark.

He set the example by tossing Bull's body upon his shoulders and setting out. The rest followed close behind him.

It was quite a job carrying the four bodies where our friends wanted to take them, especially without being seen by any one.

They made for the Hudson. In Mark's day cadets were allowed to hire rowboats, that is, all except plebes. But it was easy enough for a plebe to get one, as indeed to get anything else, tobacco or eatables. The small drum orderly is always bribable, and that accounts for the fact that two big rowboats lay tied in a quiet place, ready for the expedition.

Since the den was near the shore oars furnished an easier way to carry the prisoners to the place.

They found the boats without trouble, and deposited the yearlings in the bottom. They weren't very gentle about it, either. Then the rest scrambled in, and a long row began, during which those who were not working at the oars made it pleasant for the unfortunate yearlings by muttering sundry prophecies about tortures to come, and in general the disadvantages of being wicked. The Parson recited some dozen texts from Scripture to prove that obvious fact.

We shall not here stop to picture the infuriated Bull Harris' state of mind under this mild torture. Enough of that later. Suffice it to say the row came to an end an hour or so later, and the party stepped ashore. And also that before, they started into the woods a brilliant idea occurred to the ingeniously cruel Texas. They meant to make those cadets shiver and shake; what was the matter with letting them start now, where there was plenty of nice cold water handy?

A whispered consultation was held by the six; it was agreed that in view of all the brutality of Bull and his gang, there was no call to temper justice with mercy. As a result of that decision each one of the yearlings was held tight by the heels, and, spluttering and gasping, dipped well under water and then hauled up again. That did not cool their anger, but it made them shiver, you may well believe. During this baptismal ceremony the classic Parson was interesting, as usual. He sat on a rock nearby and told the story, embellished with many allusions, how the "silver-footed Thetis, daughter of the old man of the sea," as Homer calls her, took her son, "the swift-footed" Achilles, and dipped him into a magic fountain to give him immortality. All got wet but the heel she held him by, and so it was a blow in the heel that killed the Grecian hero.

"Therefore, gentlemen," said the Parson, "since you don't want Bull Harris to die from the treatment he gets to-night, I suggest with all sincerity that you stick him in again and wet his feet."

While this was being done, the learned Boston scholar switched off onto the subject of Baptists and their views on total immersion; which promptly reminded Dewey of a story of a "darky" camp meeting.

"Brudder Jones was very fat," said he, "and b'gee, when he got religion and wanted to be baptized there was only a little brook to put him in. They found the deepest place they could, but b'gee, Brudder Jones stomach was still out of water. Now the deacon said his 'wussest' sin was gluttony, and that if he didn't get all the way under water the devil would still have his stomach and Brudder

Jones would be a glutton all his life, b'gee. So all the brothers and sisters had to wade out into the water and sit on Brudder Jones' stomach so that all his sins would get washed away."

Those who were doing the immersing in this case were so much overcome by Dewey's way of telling that story that they almost let Baby Edwards, the last victim, slip out of their hands. But they pulled him in safely in the end, and after that the merry party set out for the "Banded Seven den."

They knew the contour of the mountains so well by this time that even in the darkness they had no difficulty in finding the place. They had relapsed into a grave and solemn silence by that time, so as to get the shivering victims into proper mood for what was next to come. Some of the crowd climbed in, and then, like so many logs of wood, the yearlings were poked through the opening in the rocks and laid on the floor inside. The rest of the plebes followed. The time for Mark's revenge had come at last.

Mark lit one of the lamps which hung from the ceiling of the cave and then went forward to make sure that everything was ready for the proposed hazing. The little room in which the bones of the trapped counterfeiters lay was up at the far end of the place. There was a heavy wall of masonry to shut it off, with only one entrance, that afforded by the heavy iron door, which was built like that of a safe. Mark entered the room and after fumbling about some came out and nodded to his companions. He did not say a word; none of them had since they had come in; but there was still that firm, set look about his mouth that boded ill for those four cowardly yearlings.

It is difficult for one to imagine the state of mind of these latter. Their rage and vexation at the failure of their scheme, at the way they had been trapped, had long since given place to one of constantly increasing dread as they felt themselves carried further and further away, evidently to the lonely mountain cave from which Bull had stolen the treasure a couple of days ago. They were in the hands of their deadliest enemies; Bull knew that they had earned no mercy from Mark, and he knew also that the wild Texan was along, the Texan to whom, as they thought, murder was an everyday affair. That dousing, too, had done its work, for it had chilled them to the bone, and made them shiver in mind as well as in body. The yearlings felt themselves carried a short way on; they felt some one test the ropes that bound them, tighten every knot, and then finally bind them to what seemed to be a series of rings in a rough stone wall. They heard a low voice whisper:

"They're safe there. They can't get near each other."

And then one by one the bandages were taken from their eyes and the gags out of their tortured mouths.

They saw nothing but the blackest of darkness. Absolutely the place was so utterly without a trace of light that the figure which stood in front to untie the gag was as invisible as if it were a spirit. Bull heard a step across the floor. But even that ceased a few moments later, and the place grew silent as the grave.

The yearlings, though their tongues were free, did not dare to whisper a word. They were too much awed in the darkness. They knew that something was coming, and they waited in suspense and dread.

It came. Suddenly the air was split by a sound that was perfectly deafening in the stillness. It was the clang of a heavy iron door, close at hand. The yearlings started in alarm, and then stood waiting and trembling. They knew then where they were, and what door that was. There was an instant's silence and then a horrified shout.

"Great Heavens! The door has slammed!"

The cadets recognized that voice; it was the mighty one of Texas, but it sounded faint and dull, as if it had passed through a heavy wall. It was succeeded by a perfect babel of voices, all of which sounded likewise. And the meaning of the voices, when once the cadets realized it, chilled the very marrow of their bones.

"Open it! Open it, quick!"

"Can't! Oh, horrors, it locks on the inside!"

"Merciful heavens! They are prisoners!"

"They'll suffocate!"

"Quick, quick, man, get a crowbar! Anything! Here, give me that!"

And then came a series of poundings upon the same iron door, accompanied by shouts and exclamations of horror and despair.

"I can't budge it. It's a regular safe. They are locked in for good!"

CHAPTER XIX

TORTURE OF THE YEARLINGS

Imagine, if you can, the state of mind of the agonized four when the import of those terrible words burst upon them. They were locked in! And tied, each one of them, so that they could not move a hand to help themselves! The darkness made the whole thing yet more awful. They were entombed alive! And suffocating! Already the air seemed to grow hot, their breath to come in choking gasps. They screamed aloud, fairly shrieked in agony. They tore at their bonds, beat upon the wall with their helpless hands and feet. And all the while outside their cries were answered by the equally terrified shouts of the plebes.

"Let us out! Let us out!" shrieked Bull.

"Can't you get loose?" they heard a voice reply; they recognized it as Mallory's. "Oh, man, you must get loose! Try! Try! We can't help you! There's a knob inside there! Turn it, turn it, and the door'll open."

"How can I turn it?" screamed Bull. "I can't get near it! I'm tied! I—oh, merciful Heaven help me! We're suffocating."

The cries from the yearlings increased in terror; outside they heard the blows of a pickax beating against the wall. Their hearts bounded in hope; they gasped in suspense; but then suddenly the sound ceased.

"I can't do a thing!" It was Texas who spoke. "The walls are too hard. We can't help them, they're gone."

"And we!" cried Mark. "Fellows, we're murderers!"

"Who knows of this yere place?" demanded Texas. "Nobody'll ever find 'em. Fellers, let's go back to camp and swear we never saw 'em."

"Oh, don't leave us! Don't leave us!" wailed Bull. "Oh! oh!"

The others joined in with their horrified shrieks, but they might as well have cried to the stones. They heard rapidly receding footsteps, and even a heartless, triumphant laugh. And a moment later there was nothing left but stone for the agonized yearlings to cry to.

The six conspirators outside, having retreated to a far corner of the cave, to talk over the success of their ruse, were considering that last mentioned point then. Indian, ever tender-hearted and nervous, wanted to let them out now, he was sure they'd dropped dead of fright; all their vociferous yells from the distance could not persuade him otherwise.

"Bless my soul!" he whispered, in an awe-stricken voice. "They'll suffocate."

"Not for an hour in that spacious compartment," said the scientific Parson.

"Anyhow, I say we let 'em out," pleaded Indian.

"An' I say we don't!" growled Texas. "That air feller Bull Harris jes' deserves to be left thar fo' good! An' I wouldn't mind doin' it, either."

Texas was usually a very mild and kind-hearted youth, but he was wont to get wroth over the very name of Harris.

"That ole yearlin's been the cause o' all our trouble an' hazin' since we come hyar!" he cried. "Ever since the day Mark caught him trying to bully a young girl, an' knocked him down fo' it, he's tried everything but murder. He's too much a coward to fight fair, but he's laid fo' us and pitched in to lick us with his gang every time he's seen us alone. He's sent Dewey and you, Mark, to the hospital! He got the yearlin's to take Mark out in the woods an' beat him.

"An' he got up that air dirty scheme to skin Mark on demerits; he did all the demeritin', besides the beatin'. An' he put up a plot to git Mark out o' bounds and dismissed. An' now I say let him stay there till he's too durnation scared to walk!"

This sentiment was the sentiment of the rest; but Mark smiled when he heard it.

"I think," he said, "it's punishment enough to stay in there a minute. We'll have to let them out pretty soon."

"An' ain't you goin' to work the other scheme?" cried Texas.

"We'll work that now," responded Mark, whispering. "See, there's the light, anyway."

This last remark was caused by a glance he had taken in the direction of the dungeon. A faint glimmer of light appeared in a crack at the top of the old, fast-falling door. And Mark arose and crept swiftly across the room.

We must go inside now and see what was going on there, for that light was destined to bring a new and startling development for the yearlings; it was what Texas had called "the other scheme."

To picture the horror of the abandoned four during the few moments that had elapsed is beyond our effort. Suffice it to say, that they were still shrieking, still despairing and yet daring to hope. And then came the new scheme.

The silence and blackness had both been unbroken except by them; but suddenly came a faint, spluttering, crackling sound. And an instant later a faint, white light shone about the narrow cell. It came from right in front of the horrified four, seeming to start in some ghostly way of its own to issue from a shining ball of no one could say what. But it was not the light, it was what it showed that terrified the cadets, and made them give vent to one last despairing shriek.

In the first place, let it be said that the light came from an inverted basket hiding a candle, set off by a time fuse the ingenious Parson had made. As for the rest, well, there were six gleaming skeletons stretched about on the floor of that horrible place, the skulls grinning frightfully, seeming to leer at the helpless victims.

The four were incapable of the least sound; their tongues were paralyzed, and their bodies too. Their eyes fairly started from their heads as they stared. They were beyond the possibility of further fright, and what came next seemed natural.

Those skeletons began to move!

First one round, white head, with its shining black holes of eyes and rows of glistening teeth, began to roll slowly across the floor. Then it sailed up into the air; then it dropped slowly down again, and finally settled in one corner and grinned out at the gasping cadets.

"Wasn't that smart of me?" it seemed to say. "I'll do it again. Watch me now. Watch!"

And it sailed up into the air once more, and swung about in the blackness and went over toward the prisoners and then started back. Finally it tumbled down to the ground, hitting its own original bones with a hollow crack. And then it was still.

That head was not the only moving thing in the cell. One skeleton raised its long, trembling arm and pointed at them; another's legs rattled across the floor. And a fourth one seemed to spring up all at once, as though it had dozens of loose bones, and hurl itself with a clatter into one corner. It lay there a scattered heap, with only one lone white rib to mark the place where it had been.

That was the way it seemed to the yearlings; of course, they did not see the black threads that ran through cracks in the door, where the six could stand and jerk them at their pleasure.

It was all over a moment later. The four heard a knob turn, and then, to their amazement, saw the iron door, which they had thought would never open on them alive, swing back and let in a flood of glorious light. And an instant later the familiar and even welcome figure of Mallory came in.

He stepped up to each and quickly cut the ropes that bound them. And when all four were free he stepped back and gazed at them. As for them, they never moved a muscle, but stared at him in consternation and confusion.

"Come out, gentlemen," said Mark. "Come out and make yourselves at home."

That voice was real, anyway, thank Heaven for that! The four had not yet succeeded in recovering their wits enough to realize the state of affairs. They followed Mark mechanically, though they were scarcely able to stand. They found themselves in the well-lit and furnished apartment, the rest of their enemies bowing cordially. Then indeed they began to realize the hoax, its success, the way they had been fooled! And they staggered back against the wall.

The silence lasted a minute at least, and then Mark stepped forward.

"Gentlemen," he said, "I hope you understand why we did this. It may seem cruel, but we could think of no other way of bringing you to your senses. We could have done much more if we had wanted to; but, we trust this will be a lesson that——"

"Confound you!" snarled Bull.

"Steady," said Mark, smiling, "or in there you go again."

That suggestion alone made Bull shiver, and he ventured not another sound.

"And now," said Mark, "if you will let us, we will conduct you back to camp. And all I want to say besides is, the next time you want to haze, try fair, open tactics. If you try any more sneaking plots I shall not show the mercy I did this time. Come on."

Some ten minutes later the four were poked through the crevice in the rocks again, and led blind-folded to the boats and to camp. Which was the end of that adventure. But Bull Harris vowed he'd get square, and that very soon.

CHAPTER XX

A NEW VENTURE

Bull Harris was resolved to "get square or die."

To "get square" was in his mind constantly, until he hit on another scheme of hazing.

It was several nights later that he and his cronies crept to the tent wherein lay Mark and three of the others.

"Don't let him move, now," whispered Bull Harris. "Hold him tight, for he'll fight like fury."

"And take that wild hyena they call Texas along, too," added another. "It was he who broke up all our fun the other night."

"He won't get a chance to use his guns this time," snarled the first speaker. "And we've got enough of a crowd to handle any of the others if they wake up. Ready, now!"

This conversation was held in a low tone off to one side. Then, having agreed just what each was to do, the crowd scattered and stole silently up to the tent.

It was important that the yearlings should not awaken the others; they placed themselves stealthily about the two victims, waited an instant, and then at the signal stooped and pinned them to the earth. The yearlings were quite expert at that now, and the two never even got a chance to gasp. They were lifted up and run quickly away, held so tight that they couldn't even kick. It was easy when there were three or four to one plebe.

The plan worked perfectly, and it seemed as if no one had discovered it. Neither of the other two sleepers had moved. Over in the next tent, however, some one was awakened by the noise, a plebe of Company B, another member of the immortal Seven. He sprang to his tent door, and an instant later found himself powerless in the grip of two yearlings who had stayed behind to watch out for just that accident. Evidently this attack was better planned than the last one.

Master Chauncey Van Rensselaer Mount-Bonsall, of Fifth Avenue, New York, was the unfortunate third prisoner. He felt himself rushed over the beat of the purposely negligent sentry and hurried into the confines of the solitary old Fort Clinton, where he was bound and gagged with celerity and precision and unceremoniously tumbled to the ground by the side of Mark and Texas.

Everything was ready for the hazing then.

The eight who had participated in that kidnaping, speedily resolved themselves into two groups of four each. The members of one group we do not know, but the other four were our old friends, Bull Harris, Gus Murray, Merry Vance and Baby Edwards. They had stepped to one side to talk over the fate of their unfortunate prisoners.

"By Heaven!" cried Bull, clinching his fists in anger. "Fellows, we've got him at last! Do you realize it, he's ours to do with as we please. And if I don't make him sorry he ever lived this night, I hope I may die on the spot."

Bull was striding up and down in excitement as he muttered this. And there was no less hatred and malice in the eyes of his three whispering companions.

"I could kill him!" cried Gus; and he said it as if he meant it.

"He's been the torment of my life," snarled Bull. "I hate him as I never hated any one, and every time I try to get square on him, somehow everything goes wrong. Just think of being penned up in a black cave with a lot of skeletons. Confound him! But he won't get away this time as he did before."

This interesting and charitable dialogue was cut short just then by one of the other four.

"What are you fellows going to do?" he cried.

"We'll be there in a moment!" whispered Bull. "Don't talk so loud. Say, fellows (this to his own crowd) I say we take Mallory off by ourselves. Those other fellows won't stand half we want to do to him."

"That's so," assented the dyspeptic Vance. "What in thunder did we let them come for?"

"We couldn't have handled Mallory and Texas alone," replied Bull, sourly. "And we had to take Texas, else he'd have waked up and followed us sure. But I guess it'll be all right. Come ahead."

The four walked over and joined the rest of the yearlings then.

"We've decided what we'll do," said Bull. "We won't need you fellows any more. We're very much obliged to you for helping us."

"Pshaw!" growled one of them. "I want to stay and see the fun."

"But there's more danger with so many away," said Bull, persuasively.

"I'll stand my share," laughed the other. "I want to stay. I've a grudge against that plebe Mallory myself."

Bull bit his lip in vexation.

"The fact is, fellows," he said, "we want to take these plebes to a place we don't know anything about."

"Why didn't you tell us that before you asked us?" growled the four. "I'm going to stay, I don't care what you say."

The fact of the matter was that the four yearlings were just a little chary about leaving their prisoner in Bull's hands, though they did not care to say so. They knew Bull Harris' character. His hatred of Mallory was well known. Who had not seen Bull, one night when the yearling class took Mallory and started to beat him into submission, seize a lash and leap at the helpless victim in a perfect frenzy of hatred. And who had not heard him all that day wrathfully telling the story of how Mallory and his gang, in an effort to cure him of his meanness, had frightened him almost to tears? Truly, thought the four, Bull's hazing was a thing to be supervised.

So they stayed, and finally Bull had to accept the situation.

"Come on," he growled, surlily.

The crowd lifted their helpless victims from the ground and set out to follow Bull's guidance. They had no idea where they were going, and in fact Bull had none himself. He could think of no form of torture that was quite cruel enough for that hated Mallory, and he did not have the brains to think of one that was as ingenious and harmless as Mallory had worked on him.

"I'd tie him up and beat the hide off him," thought Bull, "if I could only get rid of those confounded fellows that are with us. As it is, I'll have to find something else, plague take it."

The crowd had been scrambling down the steep bank toward

the river in the meanwhile. Bull thought it would be well to douse
Mallory in the water, which was one of the tricks Mallory had tried
on him. After that he said to himself it'll be time enough to think of
something more. They skirted the parade ground and made their
way down past the riding hall and across the railroad track near the
tunnel.

"I'd like to drop him on the track," thought Bull to himself, as
he heard the roar of a train approaching. "By Heaven, that would
settle him!"

The crowd had barely crossed before the engine appeared at
the tunnel's mouth, after it a long freight train slowly rumbling past
them. And at that instant Gus Murray seized Bull convulsively by
the arm.

"I've got a scheme!" he cried. "Do you hear me, a scheme?"

"What is it?" shouted Bull, above the noise of the train.

"It's a beauty," gasped Murray. "By George, we'll get 'em fired.
They'll go nobody knows where, and be missed in the morning.
And we can swear we didn't do it. Hooray! We'll put 'em on the
train!"

Bull staggered back and cried out with excitement.

"That's it!" he muttered, and an instant later, before the
horrified four could comprehend his purpose he and Edwards had
torn the helpless body of Mallory from their arms and made a rush
at a passing car. It was an empty car, and the door was half open; to
fling the plebe in was the work of but an instant; then with Murray
and Vance he quickly slid the other two in also. Half a minute later
the train was gone.

The four outsiders turned and stared at Bull's gang in horror.

"What on earth have you done?" they gasped.

And Bull chuckled to himself.

"I've sent those infernal plebes to New York," he said. "By
Jingo, I'd like to send them to Hades. If they aren't fired as it is it'll
be because you kids give us away. And now let's go back to bed."

CHAPTER XXI

MARK COMES TO TOWN

Mr. Timothy O'Flaherty was a tramp. That was the plain unvarnished statement of the case. Mr. O'Flaherty would have called himself a knight of the road, and a comic editor would have called him Tired Tim; but to everybody else he was a plain tramp.

Mr. O'Flaherty was very, very tired, having walked nearly twenty miles that day without getting even so much as a square meal. One whole pie was the sum total of his daily bread and that was so bad that he had fed it to the bulldog for revenge and walked on. He was walking still, at present on the tracks of the West Shore Railroad some thirty miles north of New York.

From what has been said of Mr. O'Flaherty you may suppose that his heart leaped with joy when along came a rumbling night freight. He watched it crawl past with a professional and critical eye; there was a platform he might ride on, but he was liable to be seen there. If only he could find an open car. There was one! He made a leap at the door, swung himself aboard with as much grace as if he had lived all his life on Broadway, and then crawled into the car.

Mr. O'Flaherty looked around. There was some one else in that car!

"Another tramp," thought the newcomer, and so to awaken him he gave him a friendly prod with his toe.

"Hello!" said he; but there was no answer.

"Drunk," was the next conjecture, but then he heard a low sound that was very much like a groan.

That scared Timothy, and he seized the figure and jerked it to the light of the moon that shone in through the door. "Be the saints!" he muttered in alarm, "it's a sojer, an' he's all tied up."

"Um—um—um!" groaned the figure in a "nasal" tone.

It was Chauncey whom the tramp had found; Chauncey had slipped into his plebe trousers before he ran to the tent door, which accounted for the man's exclamation, a "sojer." If he had found

Mark or Texas he would have exclaimed still more, for the latter two were clad in their underclothing.

Mr. O'Flaherty was a man of quick action; he saw that he couldn't gratify his curiosity about that strange traveler unless he cut him loose; so he did it.

Chauncey's first act to celebrate his liberty was a stretch and a yawn; his second was to seize the knife and rush to the back of the car, with the result that two more persons appeared in the moonlight a few minutes later.

Of Mr. Timothy O'Flaherty they did not take the least bit of notice; they appeared to have something else of much more importance to talk about just then. And Timothy sat in the shadow and stared at them with open mouth.

"Well, this is a scrape," muttered one of them, gazing at his own scantily clad figure and at the landscape rushing by.

"What kin we do?" cried a second. "The old Nick take them old yearlin's!"

"Bah Jove!" cried the third. "This is deucedly embarrassing. I cawn't go out on the street, don't cher know, dressed in this outlandish fashion!"

"And we can't get a train back," cried the first.

"An' we got no money!" said the second.

"Bah Jove!" added the third, the one Timothy recognized as "Trousers" because he was the only one who had them. "Réveille'll sound, don't cher know, and we won't be there."

This entertaining conversation was kept up for some fifteen minutes more. All Mr. O'Flaherty managed to make out was that they had been sent away from somewhere and they hadn't the least idea how to get back. Presently one of them—Trousers—discovered that he did have some money, plenty of it, whereupon Timothy's mouth began to water. That cleared the situation in his eyes, but it didn't seem to in theirs. They were afraid of being late and getting caught by some wild animal called réveille; moreover, they couldn't take a train because they had no clothes. Here Timothy thought he'd better step in.

"Hey, Trousers!" said he.

The "dude" thus designated didn't recognize himself, so Timothy edged up and poked him to make him look.

"Hey, Trousers!" said he. "I kin git you ducks some togs."

To make a long story short the "ducks" "tumbled" to that proposition in a hurry. Even Trousers, the aristocrat, condescended to sit down and discuss ways and means with that very sociable tramp. To make the story still shorter Timothy propounded a plan and found it agreeable; "jumped" the car when it was finally switched off at Hoboken; and set out with ten dollars of the stranger's money, to buy second-hand clothing at one o'clock in the morning.

"You'll be sure to come back," said Mark. "Because we'll make it fifteen if you do."

That settled whatever idea of "taking a sneak" was lurking in the messenger's mind. He vowed to return, "sure as me name is Timothy O'Flaherty," which, as we know, it was. And he came too. He flung a pile of duds into the car and went off whistling with the promised reward of virtue in his pocket. It was a "bully graft" for him anyhow, and he promised himself a regular roaring good time. That is the last we shall see of Timothy.

As to the plebes their joy was equally as great. They felt that this hazing was the supreme effort of the desperate Bull Harris, and it failed. Now that they were safe they could contemplate the delight of turning up smiling at réveille to the consternation of "the enemy." Truly this involuntary journey had panned out to be a very pleasant affair indeed.

Mark's first thought was as to a return train. They rushed off to the depot to find out, where they discovered a ticket agent who gazed doubtfully at their soiled and ragged clothing. The three realized then for the first time that their benefactor had kept a good deal of that ten dollars for himself, and poor Chauncey, to whom a wilted collar was agony, fairly groaned as he gazed at himself. However, they found that there was a train in ten minutes; and another at three-thirty-due at West Point at four-thirty-eight. That was the essential thing, and the three wandered out to the street again.

"We mustn't go far, don't cher know," observed Chauncey. "We don't want to miss that train."

Chauncey's was not a very daring or original mind. There was an idea floating through Mark's head just then that never occurred to Chauncey; it would have knocked him over if it had.

"When we went up there to West Point," began Mark, suddenly, "we expected to stay there two years without ever once venturing off the post."

"Yes," said Chauncey. "Bah Jove, we did."

"And here we are down at Hoboken, opposite New York."

"Yes," assented Chauncey again.

"It feels good to be loose, don't it?" observed Mark.

And still Chauncey didn't "tumble"; Texas' eyes were beginning to dance however.

"It's awfully stupid back there on the reservation, not half as lively as New York."

Still Chauncey only said "Yes."

"Rather kind of the yearlings to give us a holiday, wasn't it?" observed Mark.

Another "Yes," and then seeing that his efforts were of no use Mark came out with his proposition.

"Stupid!" he laughed. "Don't you see what I mean? I'm not going back on that first train."

"Not going back on that train!" gasped Chauncey. "Bah Jove! then what——"

His horrified inquiries were interrupted by a wild whoop from the delighted Texas. Texas was beginning to wriggle his fingers, which meant that Texas was excited. And suddenly he sprang forward and started down the street, seizing his expostulating companion under the arm and dragging him ahead as if he had been a child.

Some ten minutes later those three members of the Banded Seven—B. B. J.—were on a Christopher Street ferryboat bound for New York and bent upon having some "fun." When the Seven set out for fun they usually got it; they had all they could carry in this case.

It was with a truly delicious sense of freedom that they strolled about the deck of that lumbering boat. Only one who has been to West Point can appreciate it. Day after day on that army reservation, with a penalty of dismissal for leaving it, grows woefully monotonous even to the very busy plebe. Zest was added to their venture by the fact that they knew they were breaking rules and might be found out any moment.

"Still if we are," laughed Mark, "we can lay the blame on Bull. And now for the fun."

They half expected the fun would come rushing out to welcome them the moment they got into the light of the street. They expected a fire or a murder at the very least. And felt really hurt because they met only a sleepy hack driver talking to a sleepy policeman. And an empty street car and a few slouchy-looking fellows like themselves lounging about a saloon. However it was exciting to be in New York anyway; what more could the three B. J. plebes want?

They strolled across Christopher Street, gazing curiously. Mark had never been in New York before and Chauncey was worried because he couldn't see a better part of it, for instance, "my cousin, Mr. Morgan's mansion on Fifth Avenue, don't cher know." He even offered to take Mark up there, until he chanced to glance at his clothing. Then he shivered. Truly the three were a sight; Chauncey's shapely plebe trousers were hidden in a huge green threadbare overcoat (August)! Mark could not help laughing whenever he gazed at the youthful aristocrat.

"Never mind," he laughed. "Cheer up, nobody'll try to rob us, which is one comfort."

"I wish we would get robbed," growled Texas. "Whar's that aire fun we came fo'?"

That began to be a pressing question. They wandered about for at least half an hour and the clocks showed two, and still nothing had happened. The city seemed to be provokingly orderly that night.

"Durnation!" exclaimed Texas. "I reckon we got to make some fun ourselves."

When a person is really looking for excitement, it takes very little to have him imagine some. The three had just been discussing the possibility of robbery down in this "tough" quarter when suddenly Mark seized the other two by the arm.

"Look, look!" he cried.

The others turned; and straightway over the whole three of them flashed the conviction that at last their hour had come. There was a burglar!

The three started in surprise, and a moment later they slid silently into the shadow of an awning to watch with palpitating hearts.

There was only one burglar. That is, he had no confederates visible. But his own actions were desperate enough for two. In the first place he crept softly up the steps of the house, stooping and crouching as he did so. He tried the door softly, shook it; and then finding it resisted his purpose he stole down again, glancing about him nervously.

He went down into the area, where it was dark; the three, trembling by this time, peered forward to watch him. They saw him try the window and to their horror saw it go softly up. The next moment the man deliberately sat down and removed his shoes. The plebes could see them in his hands as he arose again and with the stealthiness of a cat slid quickly in.

The three hesitated not a moment, but rose up and crept silently and swiftly across the street. Mark stole down into the area, his heart beating high. He peered in and a moment later beckoned the others. They came; they saw the burglar in the act of striking a light and creeping up the basement stairs. In an instant more he was gone.

"What shall we do?" whispered the three. "What?"

Mark answered by an act. There was only one thing he could do; he stooped and crept in at the window. The three followed him immediately and their forms were lost in the darkness of that imperiled house.

CHAPTER XXII

BURGLAR HUNTING

It was an uncanny business wandering about a dark house at night; it is especially so if it be a strange house and if one knows for certain that there is a desperate burglar creeping about somewhere in it. Many a man has shrunk from that task; but the three had been bemoaning a lack of excitement, and now here it was. So they had no right to complain.

Mark waited a moment for the others to join him and then side by side they stood and peered into the darkness. From what they had seen of the room when the man struck a light it was a dining-room with a flight of stairs running up from it. Up those stairs the man had gone; and a few moments later the three cadets were standing hesitatingly at the foot of them.

"He may have a gun," whispered Chauncey.

Texas reached around to his hip pocket instinctively at that; he groaned when he realized his defenseless condition.

"That's the worst o' these yere ole Eastern ways," he muttered. "Ef a feller had bought these yere pants in Texas more'n likely he'd 'a' found some guns in 'em."

Texas had but a few moments more to growl however, for Mark stepped forward, suddenly and started up the steps.

"Come on," he said. "Let's have it over with. He can't shoot all of us at once."

Slowly they crept up the stairs, pausing at every step to listen. They reached the top and peering around found a dimly-lit hall without a sign of life about it.

"Perhaps he's in one o' them aire rooms," whispered Texas. "I——"

"S'h!" muttered Mark.

His exclamation was caused by a slight noise on the floor above, a faint tread.

"He's upon the next floor!" gasped the three. "Shall we——"

They did; Mark led the way and with still more trembling

caution they stole on, crouching in the shadow of the banisters, trying to stifle the very beatings of their hearts and breathing fast with excitement.

Up, up. There were twenty-one stairs to that flight; Mark knew that, because they stopped a long while on each listening for another clew to the burglar's whereabouts, and trembling as they imagined him peering over at them.

Not a sign of him did they see or hear, however, until they reached the level of the floor, where they could lean forward and look around the balustrade. First they heard a sound of heavy breathing, as from a sleeper. That was in the rear room, and Mark, peering in, saw the person clearly.

There was a faint light in the room, a light from a dimly-burning gas jet. The room was apparently deserted except for the sleeper. It was a woman, for Mark could see her hair upon the pillow. But where was the burglar?

The answer came with startling suddenness, suddenness that precipitated a calamity. The room next to the rear one was dark and silent until, without a moment's warning, all at once a light flashed out. And there was the burglar. The reckless villain had lit the gas, so sure was he of his safety. And he was standing now in the middle of the floor, stealthily taking off his coat before starting to work.

Naturally that sudden flash of light startled the three; it startled them so much that Chauncey leaped back with a gasp of alarm; and a moment later, his heel catching in the end of his huge green overcoat, he tripped and staggered, clutched wildly at nothing, and with a shriek of alarm tumbled backward, rolling over and over with a series of crashes that made the building shake. And then there was fun.

In the first place, as to the burglar; he started back in horror, realizing his discovery; in the second place, as to the woman; she sat up in bed with the celerity of a jack-in-the-box, and an instant later gave vent to a series of screams that awoke the neighborhood.

"Help! Help! Burglars! Murder! Thieves! Fire! Help!"

In the third place, as to the cadets. Their first thought was of Chauncey, and they turned and bounded down the steps to the bottom. They found him "rattled" but unhurt, and they picked him up and set him on his feet. Their second thought was of the burglar, that ruthless villain who perhaps even now was making his escape by a window. The thought made them jump.

"Forward!" shouted Mark.

And to a man they sprang up the stairs, two or three steps at a time, shouting "Burglars!" as they went. They reached the top and bounded into the room, where they found the man in the very act of rushing out of the door. Mark sprang at him, seized him by the throat and bore him to the ground. And the two others plunged upon the pile.

"Hold him! Hold him! Help! Help!" was the cry.

Meanwhile the woman had arisen from the bed, very naturally, and was now rushing about the hall in typical angelic costume, occasionally poking her head out of the windows and shrieking for burglars and help, using a voice that had a very strong Irish brogue.

In response to her stentorian tones help was not slow in arriving. A crash upon the door was heard; the door gave way, and up the stairs rushed two men.

"Help us hold him!" roared Texas, who was at this moment trying his level best to push the criminal's nose through the carpet. "Help us to hold him!"

But to his infinite surprise the two newcomers made a savage rush on him, and in an instant more the true state of affairs flashed over Texas.

"They're friends of the burglar!" he cried. "Whoop! Come on, thar!"

The two men were not slow to accept his invitation. They added their bodies to the already complicated heap of arms and legs that were writhing about on the floor, and after that the mêlée was even livelier than ever. Even the woman took a hand; her Irish blood would not let her stay out of the battle long, and she pitched in with a broom, whacking everything promiscuously.

What would have been the end of all this riot I do not pretend to say; I only know that Mark was devoting himself persistently to the task of holding the burglar underneath him, in spite of all manner of punches and kicks, and that Texas was dashing back and forth across the room, plowing his way recklessly through every human being he saw when the "scrap" was brought to an untimely end by the arrival of one more person.

This latter was a policeman, a policeman of the fat and unwieldy type found only in New York. He had plunged up the stairs, club in hand, and now stood red and panting, menacing the crowd.

"Stop! stop!" he cried. "Yield to the majesty of the la-aw."

Every one was glad to do that, as it appeared; the battling ceased abruptly and all parties concerned rose up and glared at each other in the dim light.

"What's the meaning of this?" cried the "cop."

If he had realized the terrible consequence of that question he would never have asked it. For each and every person concerned sprang forward to answer it.

"There's the burglar!" cried Mark, pointing excitedly at the original cause of all the trouble, who was wiping his fevered brow with diligence. "There's the burglar! Arrest him!"

"Yes, yes!" roared Texas. "Grab him! I'll tell you how it was—"

"Howly saints!" shrieked the woman, "don't let them get away! They've broken me head, in faith! An' look at me poor husband's oi!"

"Me a burglar!" roared the person thus alluded to by Mark, shaking one fist at Mark and the other at the officer. "So it's a burglar they call me, is it? So that's their trick, be jabbers! An' a foine state of affairs it is when a man can't come into his own house without being called a burglar, bad cess to it. Bridget, git me that flat-iron there an' soak the spalpeen! Be the saints!"

During that tirade of incoherent Irish the three cadets had suddenly collapsed. The situation had flashed over them in all its horror and awfulness. The "burglar" lived in the house! The woman was his wife! And they were the burglars!

The three gazed at each other in consternation and sprang back instinctively. The policeman took that for a move to escape and he whipped out his revolver with a suddenness that made Texas' mouth water.

"Stop!" he cried.

His command received even more emphasis from the fact that another policeman rushed up the stairs at that moment. The three stopped.

"See here, officer," said Mark, as calmly as he could. "This is all a mistake. We aren't burglars; we are perfectly respectable young men— —"

"You look like it," put in the other, incredulously.

Mark's heart sank within him at that. He glanced at his two companions and realized how hopeless was their case. New rags and tatters had been added by the battle. Disheveled hair, and dirt and blood-stained faces made them about as disreputable specimens as could be found in New York. Respectable young men! Pooh!

"I could explain it," groaned Mark. "We thought this man was a burglar and we followed him in. We aren't tramps if we do look it. We are— —"

And then he stopped abruptly; to tell that they were cadets would be their ruination anyway.

"You're a lot of thaves an' robbers! Sure an' thot's what yez are!" shouted the irate "burglar," filling in the sentence and at the same time making a rush at Mark.

"Come," said the policeman, stopping him. "Enough of this. You fellers can tell your yarn to the judge to-morrow morning."

Mark gasped as he realized the full import of that sentence. It was two o'clock and their train left in an hour or two—their last chance! And they could tell their story to the judge in the morning!

The policeman jerked a pair of handcuffs from his pockets and stepped up to Mark. The latter saw that resistance was hopeless and though it was torture to him he held out his wrists and said nothing. Texas, having no gun, could do nothing less. Chauncey was the only one who "kicked," and he kicked like a steer.

"Bah Jove!" he cried. "This is an insult, a deuced insult! I won't stand it, don't cher know! Stop, I say. I won't go, bah Jove! I'll send for my father and have every man on the blasted police force fired! I— —"

The snap of the handcuffs and the feeling of the cold steel subdued Chauncey and he subsided into growls. The officer took him by the arm, saying something as he did so about an "English crook." And then the three filed downstairs, the indignant and much-bruised Irishman following and enlivening the proceedings with healthy anathemas.

That walk to the station house the three will never forget as long as they live, it was so unspeakably degrading; it was only a short way, just around the corner, but it was bad enough. Idlers and loafers fell in behind to jeer at them, scarcely giving them chance to reflect upon the desperately-horrible situation they were in.

Mark was glad when at last the door of the station house shut upon them to hide them from curious eyes. There was almost no one in here to stare at them, but a sleepy sergeant at the desk; he looked up with interest when they entered, and were marched up before him.

"What's this?" he inquired.

"Burglars," said one of the officers, briefly.

Chauncey's wrath had been pent up for some ten minutes then, and at that word it boiled over again.

"I'm no burglar!" he roared. "I tell you, you fools, I'm no burglar! Bah Jove, this is an outrage."

"Faith an' yez are a burglar!" shouted the Irishman, likewise indignant. "An' faith, Mr. Sergeant, the divils broke into me house and near broke me head, too, bad cess to 'em. An' thot, too, whin Oi'd been to the club an' were a-thryin' to git to sleep without wakin' me wife. An' faith she'll be after me wid a shtick, thot she will, to-morrer!"

"We aren't burglars, I say!" protested Chauncey. "We thought he was a burglar. We're cade——"

Here Mark gave him a nudge that nearly knocked him over; he looked up and caught sight of a spruce young man with pencil and notebook working diligently. It was a reporter and Chauncey took the hint and shut up.

"Name?" inquired the sergeant, seeing him quiet at last.

"My name, bah Jove?" exclaimed the other. "Chauncey Van Ren——"

Again Mark gave him a poke.

"Peter Smith," said Chauncey.

"And yours?"

"John Jones," said Texas.

"And yours?"

Mark glanced at the others with one last dying trace of a smile.

"Timothy O'Flaherty," said he. "You understand," he added, to ease his conscience, "they're all fictitious, of course."

The sergeant nodded as he wrote the names.

"We'll find the right ones in the Rogues' Gallery," he remarked sarcastically.

That fired Chauncey again, and he went off into another tirade of abuse and indignation, which was finally closed by the officers offering to "soak him" if he didn't shut up. Then they were led off to a cell—number seven, curiously enough. And as the door shut with a clank the three gasped and realized that it was the death knell of their earthly hopes.

CHAPTER XXIII

CHAUNCEY HAS AN IDEA

Three more utterly discouraged and disgusted plebes than our friends would be hard to manufacture. There wasn't a ray of hope, any more than a ray of light to illumine that dark cell. There was only one possibility to be considered, apparently—they would be hauled up in the police court the next morning and required to give an account of themselves. If they gave it, said they were cadets, it would be good-by West Point; for they had broken a dozen rules. If on the other hand they chose to remain Peter Smith, John Jones and Timothy O'Flaherty, young toughs, it would be something like "One thousand dollars' bail," or else "remanded without bail for trial"—and no West Point all the same!

The three had characteristic methods of showing their disgust. Texas had gone to sleep in a corner, seeing no use in worrying. Mark was sitting moodily on the floor, trying his best to think of something to do. Chauncey was prancing up and down the cell about as indignant as ever was a "haughty aristocrat," vowing vengeance against everybody and everything in a blue uniform as sure as his name was Chaun—er, Peter Smith.

Mad and excited as Chauncey was, it was from him that the first gleam of hope came. And when Chauncey hit upon his idea he fairly kicked himself for his stupidity in not hitting on it before. A moment later his friends, and in fact the whole station house, were startled by his wild yells for "somebody" to come there.

An officer came in a hurry thinking of murder or what not.

"What do you want?" he cried.

"Bah Jove!" remarked our young friend, eying him with haughty scorn that made a hilarious contrast with his outlandish green August overcoat. "Bah Jove, don't be so peremptory, so rude, ye know!"

"W—why!" gasped the amazed policeman.

"I want to know, don't ye know," said Chauncey, "if I can send a telegram, bah Jove?"

"Yes," growled the other. "That is, if you've got any money."

Chauncey pulled out his "roll," which had been missed when they searched him, and tossed a five-dollar bill carelessly to the man.

"Take that," said he. "Bah Jove, I don't want it, ye know. Come now, write what I tell you."

The man took the bill in a hurry and drew out a pencil and notebook, while Chauncey's two fellow-prisoners stared anxiously. Chauncey dictated with studied scorn and indifference.

"Am—arrested," said he, "for—burglary—ye—know."

The policeman wrote the "ye know," obediently, though he gasped in amazement and muttered "lunatic."

"Under—name—of—Peter—Smith—   — —   Street—station. Come—instantly Chauncey."

"Who shall I send it to?" inquired the "stenographer."

"Let me see," Chauncey mused. "Bah Jove, not to fawther, ye know. They'd see the name, ruin the family reputation. A deuced mess! Oh yes, bah Jove, I'll have all me uncles, ye know! Ready there? First, Mr. Perry Bellwood, — — Fifth Avenue——"

"What!" gasped the officer.

"Write what I say," commanded Chauncey, sternly; "and no comments! Second, Mr. W. K. Vanderpool, — — Fifth Avenue. Third—bah Jove—Mr. W. C. Stickhey, — Fifth Avenue. Fourth—"

"How many do you want?" expostulated the other.

"Silence!" roared the "dude." "Do as I say! I take no chances. Fourth, Mr. Bradley-Marvin, — — Fifth Avenue. And that'll do, I guess, ye know. Run for your life, then, deuce take it, and I'll give you another five if they get here in a hawf hour, bah Jove."

There was probably no more amazed policeman on the metropolitan force than that one. But he hustled according to orders none the less. Certainly there was no more satisfied plebe in the whole academy class than Mr. Chauncey Van Rensselaer Mount-Bonsall of New York. "It's all right now, bah Jove," said he. "They'll be here soon."

And with those words of comfort Chauncey subsided and was asleep from sheer exhaustion two minutes later. Though he slept, forgetful of the whole affair, there were a few others who did not sleep, messenger boys and millionaires especially.

The sergeant at the desk had had no one but one "drunk" to register during the next half hour, and so he was pretty nearly asleep himself. The doorman was slumbering peacefully in his chair, and two or three roundsmen and officers were sitting together in one corner whispering. That was the state of affairs in the police station when something happened all of a sudden that made everybody leap up with interest.

A carriage came slamming up the street at race-horse speed. Any one who has lain awake at night, or rather in the early hours of morning, when the city is as silent as a graveyard, has noticed the clatter made by a single wagon. An approaching tornado or earthquake could not have made much more of a rumpus than this one. The sergeant sat up in alarm and the doorman flung upon the door and rushed out to see what was the matter.

They were soon to learn—the driver yanked up his galloping horses directly in front of the building. At the same instant the coach door was flung open with a bang. It was an elderly gentleman who hopped out, and he made a dash for the entrance, nearly bowling the doorman over in his haste.

Now it is not often that a "swell bloke" like that visits a station house at such hours. The sergeant gazed at him in alarm, expecting a burglary, a murder, or perhaps even a dynamite plot.

"What's the matter?" he cried.

The man dashed up to the desk, breathless from his unusual exertion.

"My boy!" he cried. "Where is he?"

"Your boy?" echoed the sergeant. "Where is he? What on earth?"

The sergeant thought he had a lunatic then.

"My boy!" reiterated the man excitedly. "Chauncey! He's a prisoner here!"

The officer shook his head with a puzzled look.

"I've got nobody named Chauncey," said he. "You've come to the wrong place."

The man happened to think of the telegram; he glanced at it.

"Oh, yes," he cried, suddenly. "I forgot. Peter Smith is the name he gave. You've a Peter Smith here!"

The sergeant gazed at the excited man in indescribable amazement.

"Peter Smith!" he stammered. "Why, yes. But he's a tramp. He's arrested for burglary, and——"

The strange gentleman was evidently angry at having been stirred out of bed so early in the morning. Moreover he was insulted at the outrageous idea of his nephew's being in a common prison house as a burglar. Altogether he was mad through, and didn't take the trouble to be cautious.

"Let him out this instant, I say," he demanded, indignantly. "How dare you——"

Now the sergeant was a pompous individual and he had no idea of being "bossed" like that by any one, whoever he might be, least of all in the presence of his men. Moreover, he was an Irishman, and this angry individual's superior way got him wild.

"Who are you?" he demanded, with more conciseness than courtesy.

"I'm Perry Bellwood," said the other with just as much asperity. "And what is more——"

"Who in thunder is Perry Bellwood?" roared the sergeant.

That took all the wind out of the elderly and aristocratic gentleman's sails.

"You don't know Perry Bellwood?" he gasped. "Perry Bellwood, the banker!"

"Never saw him," retorted the sergeant.

"And you won't release my nephew?"

"No, sir. I won't release your nephew!" roared the officer, hammering on his desk for emphasis. "I wouldn't release him for you or any other banker in New York, or the whole crowd of them together. Do you hear that? I'd like to know what you think a police sergeant is, anyhow. A nice state of affairs it would be if I had to set loose every burglar and murderer in prison because of some man who thinks he owns the earth because he is a banker."

The sergeant was red in the face from anger as he finished this pointed declaration. Mr. Bellwood was pacing up and down the room furiously. He turned upon the man suddenly when he finished.

"I'll bet you all I own," he said, "that you'll do as I say, and in an hour, too."

"And I'll bet you my job I don't," snapped the sergeant. "I'll see who's running this place——"

By that time the outraged banker had made a dash for his carriage. The outraged sergeant planked himself down on his chair and gazed about him indignantly.

"The very idea!" vowed he. "The very idea! That fellow talked to me as if he were the mayor. I'd a good mind to lock him up. I wouldn't let those burglars loose now for all Fifth Avenue."

He was given a chance to prove that last assertion of his, a good deal more of a chance than he expected when he made it. He had hardly gotten the words out of his mouth, and the rattle of the carriage had not yet died away before another one dashed up to the door.

The sergeant thought it was the same fellow back, and he got up angrily. The door was flung open and in dashed another man, even more aristocratic in bearing than the other.

"My name is Mr. Stickhey," said he, gravely, "and I've come-"

"I suppose you want to raise a rumpus about that confounded Chauncey, too!" cried the sergeant, getting red to the ends of his whiskers.

"W-why! What's this?" gasped the astonished millionaire.

"And I suppose you want me to let him go, don't you?"

"W-why!" gasped the astonished millionaire again. "What—"

"Well, if you do you might as well understand that I don't mean to do it. And you needn't be wasting any breath about it either. I've stood about all of this I mean to stand from anybody. I don't set my prisoners loose for the devil himself, and I won't for you. Now then!"

It would be difficult to describe the look of amazement that was on the dignified Mr. Stickhey's face. He stared, and then he started again.

"Why, officer!" said he. "I'm sure——"

"So'm I!" vowed the sergeant. "Dead sure! And all your talk

won't change the fact, either, that Peter Smith, or Chauncey, or whoever he is, stays where he is till morning. And the sooner you realize it the better."

The millionaire stared yet half a minute more, and then he whirled about on his heel and strode out, without another word.

"I'll see about this," said he.

The sergeant did not return to his seat; he was too mad. He pranced up and down the room like a wild man, vowing vengeance on all the dudes and bankers in existence.

"I wonder if any more of them are coming," exclaimed he. "By jingo, I just wish they would. I'm just in the humor—gee whiz!"

It was another! Yet older and more sedate than either of the others he marched in and gazed haughtily about him.

"I've a nephew——" he began; and there he stopped.

"Oh!" said the sergeant. "You have! Get out!"

"Why—er——"

"Get out!"

"What in——"

"Do you hear me? Get out of here, I say! Not a word, or I'll have you—ah! I wonder if there'll be any more of 'em."

This last was a chuckle of satisfaction as Millionaire No. 3 fled precipitately. The sergeant rubbed his hands gleefully. This sport bade fair to last all night, he realized to his great satisfaction as he faced about and waited.

He was waiting for number four to show up. He was getting madder still and this time he was fingering his club suggestively. At the very first gleam of a white shirt front he drew it and made a dash for the door.

It was Mr. Vanderpool, number four.

"Get out!" said the irate sergeant, menacingly, and he swung up his weapon. The gentleman thought he had met with a maniac; he gave one glance and then made a dash for the carriage. The officer faced about, replaced his club, and softly murmured "Next."

But the "next" never came. The sergeant got weary of pacing about and finally sat down again. Half an hour passed and he began to doze; the fun for that night was over, thought he, and laughed when he thought how mad be had been.

"I'd just like to see any Fifth Avenue dudes running this place," he muttered. "I never heard of such a piece of impertinence in my life!"

Through all this the plebes were peacefully sleeping. What poor Chauncey would have done if he had seen his four uncles insulted by that irate policeman is left to the imagination of the reader. It would most infallibly have been the death of Chauncey, and so perhaps it is just as well that he didn't awaken.

The clock over the station house door was at three. It will be remembered that the train left at three-thirty. The only train that could possibly save those unfortunate plebes. Three-thirty was the time the ferryboat left. But the station house was two miles and more from the ferry-slip. Altogether things were getting very interesting. For the sergeant dozed on, and the prisoners slept on and the clock went on to three-fifteen. It was a wonder Mark Mallory didn't have a nightmare.

It is of the nature of thunderbolts to strike swiftly. There is no parleying, no stopping for introductions, no delays. Therefore there will be none in describing what happened next.

The sergeant sat up with a start; so did the doorman, and so did everybody else in the place. There was the rattle of another carriage!

CHAPTER XXIV

BACK AGAIN

The sergeant had gotten over his anger, but he meant to be consistent, all the same. If this was another one of those "bloated aristocrats" he'd better look out for trouble, that was all.

The carriage drew up in the usual fashion, the sergeant seized his club. There was a flash of white shirt front and the sergeant made a leap for the door. The next moment he staggered back as if he had been shot. It was Millionaire No. 1, hatless and breathless, almost coatless and senseless, dragging in his wake—the captain of the precinct!

The sergeant saluted and gasped.

"I told you," cried Millionaire No. 1.

"You've a prisoner here named Smith?" cried the captain.

"Er—yes," stammered the sergeant.

"Send him here, quick!"

The poor officer was too much amazed and thunder-struck to be chagrined at his defeat. He made a rush for the cell; shouted to the prisoners; and half a minute later Chauncey, green August overcoat and all, was in his uncle's arms.

The sergeant turned to the smiling police captain.

"Allow me to present ——"

He was interrupted by a yell; Chauncey had glanced up at the clock.

"Good heavens!" he cried. "We've ten minutes to make the train!"

Chauncey, aristocratic and Chesterfieldian Chauncey, alas, I blush to record it, had forgotten in one instant that there was such a thing on earth as a rule of etiquette. He forgot that there was such a person on earth as a police captain. He never even looked at him. His two friends at his side, he made one wild dash for the door.

He was not destined to get out of it, however. During the excitement no one had noticed the approach of another white shirt front and in rushed Millionaire No. 2.

No. 2 had the chief of police!

"You've a prisoner here named Smith— —" cried the latter excitedly. "Release— —"

Just then the millionaire caught sight of Chauncey, and again there were handshakes and apologies, another scurrying toward the door.

"I can't stop, I tell you!" roared Chauncey. "I'll miss the train— quick—bah Jove, ye know, I'll be ruined—I— —"

There was another clatter of wheels at the door.

"Good gracious!" gasped the unfortunate cadet. "It's somebody else! Bah Jove! Deuce take the luck!"

Nothing has been said of the unfortunate sergeant during this. He was leaning against his desk in a state of collapse. Millionaire No. 3 had entered the room.

Millionaire No. 3 had a police commissioner!

"You've a prisoner here named Smith," cried he. "Release— —"

This time the plebes were desperate. They could stand it no longer. Chauncey had forced his way to the door and made a dash for one of the carriages.

"Drive— —" he began, and then he stopped long enough to see another carriage rush up—Millionaire No. 4. Millionaire No. 4 had somebody—Chauncey didn't know who. But the agonized sergeant did.

It was no less a personage than his honor, the mayor.

(His honor the mayor was mad, too, and you may bet the sergeant caught it.)

With that our three friends had nothing to do. They had piled into the carriage, Millionaire No. 1 with them, and likewise the captain, to make sure that they weren't arrested for fast driving. And away they rattled down the street.

"Christopher Street—seven minutes!" roared Chauncey. "For your life—bah Jove!"

After which there was fun to spare. New York streets aren't made for race tracks, and the way that carriage swayed and bumped was a caution. The driver had taken them at their word and was going for dear life. Three times the captain had to lean out of the window to quell some policeman who was shouting at them to slow up.

As for the plebes, there was nothing for them to do but sit still and wait in trembling anxiousness. Chauncey's uncle had a watch in his hand with the aid of which he told off the streets and the seconds.

"If we make it," said he, "we won't have ten seconds to spare. Faster, there, faster!"

The poor cadets nearly had heart failure at that.

"If we miss it," groaned Mark, "we are gone forever. The whole story'll come out and we'll be expelled sure as we're alive. What time did you say it was?"

"Drive, there, drive!" roared Chauncey.

All things come to an end. Those that haven't will some day. It seemed an age to the suffering plebes, but that drive was over at last. And the end of it was so terrible that they would have preferred the suspense.

The carriage was yanked up and brought to stop in front of the ferry gates just as the boat was gliding from her slip.

The look that was upon the faces of the three would have moved a Sphinx to tears. They sank back in the carriage and never said one word. It was all over. West Point was gone. To the three that meant that life was no longer worth the living.

It seemed almost too terrible to be true. Mark Mallory pinched himself to make sure he was alive; that all this dream had really happened, that he really was beyond hope.

And then suddenly the police captain gave vent to a startled exclamation and whacked his knee.

"Desbrosses Street!" he roared to the startled driver, and an instant later the carriage was speeding away down along the wharves.

Where they were going, or why, none of them had the least idea, except the captain; and he said nothing. The trip was a short one, only three or four blocks. At the end of it he sprang from the carriage.

"Quick, quick!" he cried, and made a dash for one of the piers.

The rest did not need to be urged to follow. They beat the

captain there in their haste. For they saw then where he was going; a police tug was lying at the wharf.

"Quick!" roared the captain, leaping aboard. "Follow that ferry!"

And half a minute later the engines of the tug were throbbing and the tug was sweeping out into the river.

A few minutes after that there were three tough-looking tramps contentedly dozing in a Pullman car of the West Shore express.

The same three sneaked into Camp McPherson at the very moment when Cadet Corporal Vance (of the Bull Harris gang) was superintending the loading of the réveille gun.

CHAPTER XXV

A CHALLENGE

"Hey, there, wake up!"

"Um—um. Don't bother me."

"Wow! Git up, man——"

"Say, Texas, didn't I tell you I wanted to sleep this hour? Haven't I been awake now two nights in succession helping you haze the yearlings? Now I want to take a nap; so let me alone."

"Wake up!" repeated Texas. "Ain't you got sense enough, Mark Mallory, to know I'm not pesterin' you fo' nothin'? Git yo' eyes open thar and listen. I got something to tell you. I know you're sleepy—thar ain't no need tellin' me that aire ag'in. I know you were up night afore last hazin' them ole yearlin's, an' last night, too, 'cause they tied us up an' fired us into that freight train goin' to New York. But this hyar's more 'portant than sleepin'!"

"What is it?" demanded Mark.

"There's a committee from the first class wants to see you."

"What!"

"Thar, naow! I knew you'd get yo' eyes open," laughed the other triumphantly.

"What do they want?" inquired Mark.

"You know what they want well as I do," responded Texas. "They want you. They want you 'cause you're the most B. J. plebe ever came to West Point, 'cause you dared to defy 'em, to refuse to be hazed, to lick 'em when they tried it, an' to all 'round raise the biggest rumpus this hyar ole place ever see. That's what!"

"Do you mean," laughed Mark, "that they want me to fight some more?"

"Course they do!" roared Texas. "You old idiot, you! Why ain't yo' up hustlin' fo' the chance? You don't appreciate yo' opportunity, sah. Ef I had the chance to wallop them ole cadets like you've got—wow! You know what I'd do?"

"I'm not a fire-eating, wild and woolly cowboy hunting for fight," responded Mark.

"That's all right," grinned the other. "You'll do it when the time comes. I never see you run yit when you ought to be fightin', an' neither did them ole cadets. An' say, Mark! There's fun ahead! Whoop! You remember ever since you had the nerve to go to the hop, somethin' no plebe ever dared do afore, them ole first class fellers vowed they'd make you sorry. You made 'em madder since by lickin' one of 'em when they dared you to. An' now they're comin' 'roun' to git square."

"Do you mean they're going to make me fight every man in the class, as they said?" inquired Mark.

"That's jes' what I do!" cried Texas, gleefully. "Jes' exactly! Come out hyer an' see 'em yo'self."

Mark had been making his toilet before the little looking-glass that hung on the tent pole; he turned then and accompanied his friend out of camp and over to Trophy Point, where sat in all stateliness and dignity three solemn-looking seniors, a committee from the first class to Mark Mallory, the desperate and defiant and as yet untamed "B. J." plebe. But he wasn't going to remain untamed very long if that committee had anything to do with it.

They arose at his approach.

"Mr. Mallory?" said the spokesman.

Mr. Mallory bowed.

"You come from the first class, I believe," he said. "Let us proceed right to business."

The committee, through its spokesman, cleared its throat with a solemn "Ahem!"

"Mr. Mallory," said he, "I presume you have not forgotten that a short while ago you ventured to defy our class openly. The class has not forgotten it, for such conduct in a plebe cannot be tolerated here. Your conduct ever since you came has been unbearably defiant; you have set at naught every cadet law of the academy. And therefore, as the class warned you beforehand, you must expect trouble."

Mr. Mallory bowed; he'd had a good deal of it already, he thought to himself.

"The class has been waiting," continued the other, "for you to recover from the effects of a dislocated shoulder, an injury due to another unpleasant — ahem — accident — —"

"Or, to be more specific," inserted Mark, very mildly, "due to the fact that I was — er — attacked by some — ahem — fifty members of the first class in a body."

"Not quite so many," said the chairman, flushing. "The incident is regretted by the class."

"By me also," said Mark, rubbing his shoulder suggestively.

"It appears," the other continued hurriedly, "that you are now recovered. Therefore, to be brief, the class has sent us to inquire as to your wishes concerning the duty you undertook when you ventured to defy them. You know what I mean. You stand pledged, and you will be compelled to defend yourself before every member of our class in turn until you agree to apologize and become a plebe once more."

The spokesman stopped and Mark answered without hesitation, looking him squarely in the eye.

"Tell the class," said he, "that I am ready to meet any one it may select, to-day if necessary, and in any place they choose. Tell them also if they could manage to select one of those who helped to injure my shoulder I should consider it a favor. Tell them that I have nothing to apologize for. Tell them that I renew my defiance, with all possible courtesy, of course; tell them I once more refuse to be hazed, and shall refuse even when I am beaten; and — —"

Here the excitable ex-cowboy, who had been listening with most evident delight, sprang forward with a whoop.

"An' tell 'em," he roared, "doggone their boots, ef they lick Mark fair or foul they ain't hardly begun what they'll have to do! Tell 'em, sah, there's a gennelman, what never yit run from man or devil, named Jeremiah Powers, sah, son o' the Honorable Scrap Powers, o' Hurricane County, Texas. Tell 'em he's jes' roaring for a scrap, an' that he'll start in whar Mallory quits! An' tell 'em — —"

But the committee had turned away and started across the parade ground by that time. The committee didn't consider it necessary to listen to Mr. Jeremiah Powers.

Mark had listened however; and as he took Texas by the hand the excitable Texas saw in his eyes that he appreciated the offer.

"And now," said Mark at last, "if I am to do some fighting I'd best go back and finish that nap. I'll need to make up for the sleep I've missed."

An important event had happened to that company that day, one that had made a great change in their lives. A month and a half of drill and discipline, the most rigorous possible, had been judged to have had its effect. And that day the plebes were honored by being put in the cadet battalion.

Previously they had "herded" alone, a separate roll call, separate drills, separate seats in mess hall. But now all was changed. The plebe company was broken up, the members each going to their own company in the battalion, to hear their names called with the others at roll call, to march down to meals and sit with them, too. And that afternoon for the first time the plebes were to march on parade, Mark and Texas under the command of Fischer, cadet-captain of Company A.

Concerning Fischer, the high and mighty first classman, it may be well to say a word, for he will figure prominently in this story. Fischer was a member of the first class, and its idol. Tall, handsome and athletic, he made an ideal captain; even the plebes thought that, and strange to say, our B. J. plebes most of all. For Fischer was a fair-minded, gentlemanly fellow and more than once he had interfered to see that Mallory got fair play with his enemies.

He came in that same afternoon to have a word with Mark as to the latest excitement; it was an unusual thing indeed for a cadet-captain even to speak to a plebe, but Fischer chose to be different. And, moreover, Mallory had earned for himself many privileges most plebes had never dreamed of.

"I got a letter from your friend, Wicks Merritt," said Fischer. "His furlough is coming to an end. Poor Wicks is very much agitated for fear you'll be hazed out of West Point before he gets here. But I told him there wasn't much danger. I think you'll stick."

"I shall try," laughed Mark, while Texas sat by in awe and gazed at the young officer's chevrons and sash. "I shall try. Have you heard of my engagement—the latest?"

"Yes," answered the other, "I have. That's what I came in for. I don't envy you."

"I don't myself," said the plebe thoughtfully. "I don't like to fight. I'd a thousand times rather not, and I always say 'no' when I can. But I've vowed I wouldn't stand the kind of hazing I got, and I don't mean to so long as I can see."

"I wish you luck," said Fischer. "I've told the men in my own class that, for I haven't forgotten, as they seem to, the time you rescued that girl in the river."

"Do you know who'll be the first man I meet?" inquired the other, changing the subject.

"I do not; the class is busily holding a conclave now to decide who's the best. They'll send their prize bantam the first time, though I doubt if we've a man much better than Billy Williams, the yearling you whipped. Still you've got to be at your best, I want to tell you, and I want you to understand that. When a man's been three years here at West Point, as we have, he's in just about as perfect trim as he ever will be in his life."

"So am I," responded Mark.

"You are not," said Fischer, sharply. "That's just the trouble. I wouldn't be warning you if you were. I've heard of the monkey shines you've been kicking up; Bull Harris, that good-for-nothing yearling, was blowing 'round that he'd put you on a train for New York. The whole thing is you've been losing sleep."

Mallory tried to pass the matter over lightly, but Fischer was bound to say what he'd come for.

"I suppose it's none of my business," he continued, "but I've tried to see you get fair play. And I want to say this: You rush in to fight those fellows to-day, as they'll try to make you, and you'll regret it. That's all. As the challenged party the time is yours to name. If you refuse for a week at least, I'll back you up and see that it's all right, and if you don't you'll wish you had."

Having delivered himself of which sage counsel the dignified captain arose to go. Perhaps his conscience troubled him a little anyhow that he'd stayed so long in a plebe tent.

He thought of that as he came out and espied three members of his own class coming down the street and looking at him. They hailed him as he passed.

"Hey, Fischer!"

They were three who had been the "committee"; they were a committee still, but for a different purpose. Their purpose was to see Fischer, and when he came toward them, they led him off to one side. The message that committee had to give was brief, but it nearly took Fischer off his feet.

"Fischer," said one, "the fellows have decided about that Mallory business."

"Yes," said Fischer. "What?"

"They've decided that you'll be the man to meet him first."

And the committee wondered what was the matter with Fischer.

CHAPTER XXVI

"I HAVE THE COURAGE TO BE A COWARD"

Something which happened immediately after Fischer left the tent effectually drove from Mark's mind all ideas of fights and first classmen. It was the blessed long-expected signal, a roll upon the drum, the summons to fall in for the evening's dress parade.

And oh, how those plebes were "spruced up!" The four members of the Banded Seven who roomed in Mark's tent had taken turns looking over each other in the effort to find a single flaw. A member of the guard trying for colors was never more immaculate than those anxious strangers. Of the many pair of duck trousers allotted to each cadet every pair had been critically inspected so as to get the very whitest. Buttons and belt plates were little mirrors, and every part of guns and equipments shone. When those four "turned out" of their tent they felt that they were worthy of the ceremony.

It was an honor to be in the battalion, even if you were in the rear rank and could see nothing all the time but the stiffly marching backs in front. And it was an honor to have your name called next to a first classman's on the roll. The cadet officer had known the roll by heart and rattled it off in a breath or two; but now he had to read it slowly, since the new names were stuck in, which bothered him if it did delight the plebes.

It was a grand moment when each plebe answered very solemnly and precisely to his own; and another grand moment when the cadet band marched down the long line to its place; and another when the cadet adjutant turned the parade over to the charge of the officer in command; and finally, last of all, the climax, when the latter faced about and gave the order, "Forward, march!" when the band struck up a stirring tune and amid waving of flags and of handkerchiefs from hundreds of spectators, the all-delighted plebes strode forward on parade at last.

How tremblingly and nervously he stepped! How gingerly and

cautiously he went through the manual of arms! And with what a gasp of relief he finally broke ranks at the sunset gun and realized that actually he had gotten out of it without a blunder!

Then they marched him down to supper. Formerly the plebes had marched dejectedly in the rear and sat over in an obscure corner of the room. That had its advantages, however, for he did not have to pour the water and wait till everybody else was helped, and he was not subject quite so much to the merry badinage of the merciless yearling. On the whole he was rather glad when supper was over and after marching back to camp was dismissed for that day at last.

Mark and his chum, who as we have seen were now interested in nothing quite so much as sleep, or lack of it, made for their tents immediately to go to bed. But once more the fates were against them, for scarcely had they entered the door before another cadet rushed in. It was the excited first captain, and he was in such a hurry that he had not even stopped to remove his sword and sash, the remnants of "parade." He bore the news that the committee had imparted to him; and its effect upon Mallory may be imagined.

"Fight you," he gasped. "For Heaven's sake, man, you're wild."

"I'm as serious as I ever was in my life," replied the other. "The committee from the class told me just before parade."

"What on earth made them select you?"

"I don't know," groaned Fischer. "I had a couple of fights here—I whipped Wright, the man you knocked out the time when the class attacked you so disgracefully. And they seem to think I'd stand the most chance, at least that's what the committee said."

"And what did you tell them?" inquired Mark, in alarm.

"Tell them? I haven't told them anything yet. I was too horrified to say a word. I've come over to see you about it. I'm in a terrible fix."

"Well, refuse, that's all."

"I can't!"

"But why not?" demanded Mark.

"My dear fellow," protested the other, "you don't understand how the class feels about such things. I'm a member of it, and when

I'm called upon to defend the class honor I daren't say no. When you have been here as long as I have you'll understand how the cadets would take it. They'd be simply furious."

"Then do you mean," gasped the other, staring at him in consternation, "that I'm expected to fight you?"

"I don't see what else," responded the captain, reluctantly. "What can I tell the class? If I simply say that I've been rather friendly with you, they'll say I had no business to be. And there you are."

"No business to be," echoed Mark, thoughtfully, gazing into space. "No business to be! Because I'm a plebe, I suppose. And I've got to fight you!"

"What else are we to do," protested the other. "I'm sure I shan't mind if you whip me, which you probably will."

"Whip you!" cried Mark; he had sprung to his feet, his hands clinched. And then without another word he faced about and fell to striding up and down the tent, the other watching him anxiously.

"Mr. Fischer," he demanded suddenly, without looking at the other, "suppose I refuse to fight you?"

"Don't think of it!" cried Fischer, in horror.

"Why not?"

"Because you would be sneered at by the whole corps. Because they would call you a coward and insult you as one, cut you dead! You could not stand it one week."

"What else?" inquired Mark, calmly.

"What else! What else could there be! For Heaven's sake, man, I won't have it! I couldn't make the class understand the reason. You'd be an outcast all the time you were here."

"Is that all?"

"Yes."

And Mark turned and gazed at the other, his brown eyes flashing.

"Mr. Fischer," he began, extending his hands to the other, "let me tell you what I have thought of you. You have been the one friend I have had in this academy outside of my own class and Wicks Merritt; you have been the one man who has had the fairness to give me my rights, the courage to speak for me. I have not always taken your advice, but I have always respected you and admired you. And, more than that, I owe my presence here to you."

Mark paused a moment, while his thoughts went back to the time.

"I had enemies," he continued at last, slowly, "and they had me in their power. They had persuaded the superintendent that I was a criminal, and I looked for nothing but disgrace. And it was you, then, and you only of all the cadets of this academy, who had honor and the courage to help Texas prove my innocence. And that debt of gratitude is written where it can never be effaced. My debt to you! And now they want me to fight you!"

The captain shifted uneasily.

"My dear fellow," he began, "I can stand it."

"It is not for you to stand," said Mark. "It is for me. It is I who owe the debt, and I shall not pay it with blows. Mr. Fischer, I shall not fight you."

"But what will you do? You will be reviled and insulted as a coward."

"Yes," said Mark, firmly; "I will. But as I once told Texas, there are a few things worse than being called a coward, and one of them is being one."

"I know," protested Fischer. "But then——"

"There are times," Mark continued, without heeding him, "times, I say, when to fight is wrong."

"Yes!" cried the other. "This is one."

"It is," said Mark. "And at such times it takes more courage not to fight than to fight. When an army goes out to battle for the wrong the brave man stays at home. That is a time when it takes courage to be a coward. And Mr. Fischer——"

Mark took the other by the hand and met his gaze.

"Mr. Fischer, I have the courage to be a coward."

There was silence after that, except for a muttered "Oh!" from Texas. Mark had said his say, and Fischer could think of nothing.

"Mr. Mallory," he demanded at last, "suppose you let me do the refusing?"

"It would be best for me to do it," said Mark, with decision. "Disgrace would be unbearable for you. You have your duty to your class; I have no duty to any one but myself. And moreover, I am a plebe, cut by everybody already and pledged to fight every one. To fight them a few times more will not hurt. And I really like to defy them. So just leave it to me."

That was the end of the talk. Fischer sat and looked at Mark a few moments more, feeling an admiration he did not try to express. But when he arose to go the admiration was in the grip of his hand.

"Mr. Mallory," he said. "You do not realize what you attempt. But you may rest assured of one thing. I shall never forget this, never as long as I live. Good-night."

And as the captain's figure strode up the street Mark turned and put his hands on Texas' shoulders.

"Old fellow," said he, "and have you any courage?"

"Say," protested Texas, solemnly, "I'll fight— —"

"I don't mean that kind of courage," said Mark. "I mean courage of the eye, and the heart. Courage of the mind that knows it's right and cares for nothing else. I mean the courage to be called a coward?"

"I dunno," stammered Texas, looking uneasy. Poor Texas had never thought of that kind of courage. "I ain't very sho'," he said, "'bout lettin' anybody call me a coward."

"That is what I mean to do," said Mark. "I mean to let them call it, and look them in the eye and laugh. And we'll see what comes of it. I won't fight Fischer, and they can't make me. The more they taunt me, the better I'll like it. When they get through perhaps I'll get a chance to show them how much of a coward I am."

With which resolution Mark turned away and prepared for bed.

CHAPTER XXVII

MARK, THE COWARD

The taunting of which Mark spoke with such grim and quiet determination was soon to begin; in fact, he was not destined to lie down for that night of rest without a taste of it. He had barely removed the weight of his uniform jacket, with its collar fastened inside, before he heard a sound of voices near his tent.

He recognized them instantly; it was the "committee," and a moment later, in response to his invitation, the three first classmen entered, bowing most courteously as usual.

"Mr. Mallory," said the spokesman, "I have come, if you will pardon my disturbing you, to deliver to you the decision of our class."

"Yes," said Mark, simply. "Well?"

It was evident that Fischer had not seen them, and that they suspected nothing. A storm was brewing. Mark gritted his teeth.

"It might just as well come now as any time," he thought. "Steady!"

"The class will send a man to meet you this evening in Fort Clinton," said the cadet.

"Ah," responded Mark. "Thank you. And who is the man?"

"He is the captain of your company, Mr. Fischer. And that is about all, I believe."

"It is not all," observed Mark, very quietly; and then, as the other turned in surprise, he clinched his fists. "I refuse to fight Mr. Fischer," he said.

"Refuse to fight him?"

The three gasped it all at once, in a tone of amazement that cannot be shown on paper.

"And pray," added the spokesman, "why do you refuse to fight Mr. Fischer?"

"My reasons," said Mark, "are my own. I never try to justify my conduct to others. I simply refuse to fight Mr. Fischer. I'll fight any other man you send."

"You'll fight no one else!" snapped the cadet. "Mr. Fischer is the choice of the class. If you refuse to meet him, and give no reason, it can only be because— —"

"Because you know he's too good a man for you!" put in one of the others. "Because you're afraid of him!"

Mark never winced at that; he gave the man a look straight in the eye.

"There are some people," he said, "I am not afraid of. I am not afraid of you."

The cadet's face turned scarlet, and he clinched his fists angrily.

"You shall pay for that," he cried. "You— —"

But the spokesman of the committee seized him and forced him back.

"Shut up, old man," he exclaimed. "Don't you see what he's trying to do. He's afraid of Fischer, and he's trying to force a fight with some one else. He's a dirty coward, so let him alone."

Mark heard that plainly, but he never moved a muscle. It was too much for our tinder-box Texan, however; Texas had been perspiring like a man in a torture chamber during this ordeal, and just then he leaped forward with a yell.

"You ole white-faced coyote, you, doggone your boots, I'll—"

"Texas!" said Mark, in his quiet way.

And Texas shut up like an angry oyster and went back into the corner.

"Now, gentlemen," said Mark, "I think our interview is at an end. You understand my point. And that is all."

"And as for you," retorted the other. "Do you understand your position? You will be branded by the cadets as a coward. You will fight Fischer as sure as the class can make you. And you will fight no one else, either, until you fight him."

Mark bowed.

"And you'll allow me to express my opinion of you right here," snapped the insulted one, who was going to fight a moment ago. "You needn't get angry about it, either, because you've no redress till you fight Fischer. You're a coward, sir! Your whole conduct since you came here has been one vulgar attempt to put up a bluff with nothing to back it. And you lack the first instincts of a gentleman, most of all, sir, because you'll swallow such insults from me instead of fighting, and taking the licking you've earned. You can't fight me till you've fought Fischer."

"Can't, hey! Say, d' you think I'm a-goin' to stan' sich — —"

"Texas!"

And once more there was quiet, at the end of which the indignant committee faced about without a word and marched out in disgust.

"He's not worth fooling with," said the spokesman, audibly. "He's a coward."

After which Mark turned to Texas and smiled.

"That was the first dose, old man," said he. "How did you like it?"

From Texas' face he liked it about as well as a mouthful of quinine, and if Texas hadn't been very, very sleepy he would probably have lain awake all night growling like an irate volcano, and wondering how Mark could snore away so happily while such things were happening.

Though Mark slept, there were no end of others who didn't sleep on account of him. The committee, just as soon as they had gotten outside, had rushed off to tell the story of "Mallory's flunk," and pretty soon there were groups of first classmen and yearlings standing about the camp indignantly discussing the state of affairs. There were various opinions and theories, but only one conclusion:

That plebe Mallory's a coward!

Fischer was not there to gainsay it, he being absent on duty, and so the cadets had no one to shed any light on the matter, which they continued to rave about right up to the time for tattoo. The first class was so worked up over it that there was an impromptu meeting gathered to discuss it just outside of the camp.

The angry mob was reduced to an orderly meeting a little later by the president of the class, who appeared on the scene and called the cadets to order to discuss ways and means of "swamping Mallory." For every one agreed that something ought to be done that very night. As has been stated, they never dispersed until the very moment of tattoo; by that time they had their campaign mapped out. It was a very unpleasant programme for poor Mark.

He had to dress and turn out, of course, at tattoo to answer to his name before he retired for the night. Not a word was said to him then; yet he could see by the angry looks and frowns he met with that the story of his conduct was abroad. But Mark had not the least idea of what was coming, and he went back to his tent and fell asleep again in no time.

It is an old, old story, an old, old incident. To tell it again would weary the reader. That night a dozen men, chosen by the class for their powerful build, instead of going to sleep when taps sounded, lay awake and waited till the camp got quiet. They waited till the tac had gone the rounds with his lantern, and then to his tent for the night. They waited till the sentry's call had been heard for the fourth time since taps.

"Twelve o'clock and all's we-ell!"

They they got up and dressed once more, and stole silently out into the darkness of the night. Outside, in the company street, they met and had a whispered consultation, then surrounded a certain "plebe hotel" and finally stole away in triumph, bearing four helpless plebes along with them. A while later they had passed the sentry and had their victims bound and gagged, lying in a lonely corner of old Fort Clinton.

The cadets thought four would be enough that night. They meant to give those plebes the worst licking they had ever had in their lives. That would be a pretty severe one, especially for Mallory, who had been roughly handled before. But the first classmen had agreed among themselves that there was no call for mercy here.

The reader may perhaps wish to be spared the details of the preparation. Suffice it to say that those heavily bound unfortunates were stretched out upon the ground, that their backs were bared, and then that the four brawniest of the desperate cadets took four pieces of rope in their hands and stepped forward. It was estimated that when they stepped back those four plebes would be in a more docile mood than previously.

A dead silence had fallen upon the group; it had increased in numbers every moment, for other cadets had stolen out to see what was being done. And just then every one of them was leaning forward anxiously, staring at Mallory, for nobody cared anything much about the other three, whether they were attended to or not. It was Mallory, the coward, against whom all the hatred was; Mallory, whom the biggest man had been deputed to attend to. All the other "executioners" were waiting, leaning forward anxiously to see how Mallory took it.

The cadet who held the rope seized it in a firm grip, and swung it about his head. A moment later it came down through the air with a whirr. It struck the white flesh of the helpless plebe with a thud that made the crowd shudder. A broad red streak seemed to leap into view, and the victim quivered all over. The cadet raised the lash once more and once more brought it down; and again an instant later.

The end of it came soon, fortunately; and it came without waiting the wish of the "hazers."

Once before that game had been tried on Mallory, then by the infuriated yearlings. An alarm from camp had interrupted it at an earlier stage. And that happened again. This time there broke upon the stillness of the midnight air the sharp report of a gun. It came from nearby, too, and it brought no end of confusion with it, confusion that will be told of later.

As to the hazers, they glanced at each other in consternation. That gun would awaken the camp! And they would be discovered! There was not a second to lose!

In a trice the four plebes were cut loose, left to get back to their tent as best they could; and a few moments later a mob of hurrying figures dashed past the sentry and into Camp McPherson, which they found in an uproar. The hazing of Mallory was over for that night beyond a doubt.

CHAPTER XXVIII

A TEST OF COURAGE

The story of the sacred geese that saved the city of Rome is known to every schoolboy. Not so long ago the classic Parson, of the Banded Seven, told of a spider who saved the life of Bruce the Scot, by building a web over the entrance of the log he hid in. As life-savers, dogs and even horses are famous, too, but it is left to the historian of these pages to tell of how a rescue was effected by a mouse.

Perhaps you think to be told it was a mouse who fired that gun and saved Mark. Well, in a sense it was true.

The mouse who is our hero lived in the West Point Hotel, situated a very short way beyond the camp. And the tale of his deed, unlike the mouse's tail, is a very short one. It was simply that some one left a box of matches upon a table in the kitchen, and that the mouse got after those matches. There you have it.

Some of them fell to the floor, and the mouse went after them. He bit one, after the fashion of inquisitive mice; then, scared at the result, turned and scampered off in haste. Inquisitive persons sometimes make no end of trouble.

There was a piece of paper near the match, and then more paper, and the leg of the table. There was also plenty of time and no one to interfere. Every one who was in that building, except the clerks and the watchman in the office, was sleeping soundly by that time of night, and so the small crackling fire was in no hurry. It crept up the leg of the table, its bright forked tongues dancing about gayly as it did so. Then it leaped over to a curtain at the window, and then still more swiftly to the window frame, and still there was no one to see it.

Quietly at rest in that hotel, and unsuspecting, were some dozens of guests, including one that interests us above all others, Grace Fuller. Her room was now on the top floor of the hotel, and in the corner of the building that was fast getting warm and choking.

It is a horrible thing, the progress of a fire through the still watches of the night. Creeping ahead and crackling it goes, so slowly and yet with such deadly and inevitable purpose. It has been called a devouring fiend; it has greedy tongues that steal on and lick up everything, and grow hungrier and more savage as they feed. And it breathes forth volumes of deep black poison that stupefy its victims till it comes to seize them.

The unguarded kitchen of the hotel was soon a roaring furnace, and then the fire crept out into the hall, and as the glass of the windows cracked and a rush of fresh air fanned in, the flames leaped up the staircase as if it had been the chimney, and then spread through the parlor, and on upward, farther and farther still. And how were people to get down those stairs if they did not hurry about it?

The people were not thinking of that; they were not even beginning to have bad dreams until the smoke got just a little thicker, until the halls outside got just a little hotter, until the fire had moved on from the basement to the ground floor, and from the ground floor to the next above. And even then they were not destined to discover it. That task was left to some one else.

It was a sentry, a sentry of the regular army, facing the walk called Professor's Row. That sentry had no business to leave his post, but he did it none the less, and dashed across the street to look, as he caught sight of that unusual glare from the windows of the old hotel. An instant later he had swung up his musket to his shoulder, snapped back the trigger, and then came the roar of the gun that the startled cadets had heard from the deep recesses of the fort.

The sentry, the instant he had fired, lowered the gun, snapped out the cartridge, and slid in another to fire again. Before the camp had gotten its eyes open a third report had come also, the dreaded signal of fire. The sentry had done his duty then, and he set out once more to march back and forth upon his post.

The wild excitement that ensued it is impossible to picture; everything in camp was moving and shouting at once. Lieutenant Allen, the tac of Company A, on duty for the night, had leaped from his bed at the first bang, and from his tent at the second. His yell for the drum orderly brought that youngster out flying, and the third report of the gun was echoed by a rattle of drums that seemed never to stop. It was the dreaded "long roll."

Cadets sleep in their underclothing, like firemen, ready for just such an emergency as this. They were springing into their clothing before they were entirely awake, and rushing out to form in the company street before they were half in their clothing. Those who had been into Fort Clinton were the first in line, and as the others followed they heard the cadet adjutant rattling through the list of names, and Lieutenant Allen shouting orders as if trying to drown the other's mighty voice. And above it all rang shrieks and cries from the now awakened inmates of the building, the glare of the fire shining through the trees.

It was the matter of but a minute or two for the company fire battalion to be out and ready for duty. But at such times as these seconds grow to hours. Fischer, out of his tent among the first, and quick to think, spoke a few words to the lieutenant, and at his nod dashed on ahead with the cadets from the guard tent at his heels. And it is Fischer we must follow now.

Things were happening with frightful rapidity just then. Fischer and his little command, when they got there, found that fully half the occupants of the place had managed to get out already. They had gotten a ladder and were raising it to the piazza roof. Up that ladder the cadets rushed, and then raised it after them and put it up to the next floor and sped on. Into the smoke-laden rooms they dashed, and through the glaring flames in the halls, pausing at nothing, hearing nothing but the ringing commands of their leader. There was work for the members of the guard detail that night, and glory for Fischer.

They were still at work helping women and children out when the battalion put in an appearance, coming on the double-quick with a cheer of encouragement. They bore buckets and more ladders, and behind them, still faster, clattered the members of the cavalry company of the post. The two bodies reached the scene at about the same instant, and each went to work with a will.

The white uniforms of the cadets shone in the yellow glare of the flames; there were some pale faces staring into that light and some trembling knees. But there was no trembling or hesitating among the officers in command. They had the pumps working, and long lines of bucket passers formed in no time. And there were ladders at the windows and details of cadets searching the smoke-laden rooms.

The work of rescue was nearly over, however, by the time the battalion got there, thanks to the fearless efforts of the first captain's prompt little band. Fischer had thought all were out, and had settled down to emptying water on the flames, when the alarm we have to do with was given.

It came from a white-haired figure, an old gentleman, who rushed up breathless and panting to the scene. Every one recognized him, and started in horror as they heard his cry. It was Judge Fuller.

"My daughter! My daughter!" he shrieked. "Oh, save her!"

He rushed to one of the ladders, about to spring into the very center of the flames. Several of the cadets forced him back, and at the same instant a ringing cheer broke from the whole battalion. It was Fischer once more; he had been standing on the roof when he heard the cry, and like a flash he had turned and bounded in at the window. He was lost then to view, swallowed up in the smoke and flames. And, scarcely breathing, the crowd outside stood and stared at the windows and waited.

Perhaps you are asking what of Mark, with Grace Fuller, the joy of his life, in peril. Mark was down in the long line, passing buckets like any dutiful plebe. He had heard Judge Fuller's terrible warning, and had been quick to spring forward. But the watchful "tac" had had his eye on Mark, knowing his friendship for the girl. Lieutenant Allen did not mean to have his lines broken up in that way; there were others to attend to that rescue, and he ordered Mallory back to his place with a stern command that Mallory dared not disobey. Now he was standing like a warrior in chains amid the battle's roar, watching with the rest, and trembling with horror and dread.

What if Fischer should fail—be beaten back? What if smoke should overcome him, and he should sink where he was? What if Grace Fuller——

And then, oh, how he did gasp for joy! And what a perfect roar of triumph rose from the anxious crowd. There was the gallant captain, smoke-stained and staggering, standing in a window on the top floor, holding in his arms a figure white as snow. The girl was safe!

But how was she to get down?

That was the dreadful thought that flashed over the trembling cadet. They stood irresolute, and so did the cadet in the window, hesitating at times when a second might mean the difference between life and death.

And yet who could advise him? The girl's waving hair and dress would catch at the slightest flame; to try the roaring staircase was suicide. Then should he drop her? The crowd shuddered to think of that, yet what else could he do? There was no ladder to reach halfway. He must! He was going to!

Picture the state of Mark Mallory's mind at that moment. Himself helpless, watching Fischer preparing for that horrible deed. He saw the cadet drag a half-blazing mattress from one of the rooms, laying it on the roof below. He heard the agonized shriek of the girl's father, he pictured that lovely figure perhaps dying, certainly maimed for life. He saw Fischer passing the body through the window, his figure wreathed in smoke, with a setting of fire behind. And then, with a shout that was a perfect roar of command, Mark leaped forward.

"Stop! Stop!"

A thousand tacs could not hold him then; he was like a wild man. He saw a chance, a chance that no one dared. But he—what was he, compared with perfection, Grace Fuller?

He fairly tore a path up the ladder.

He paused but an instant on the roof of the piazza, to shout to Fischer, then seized in his hand a rope that some were vainly trying to toss up to the window. That rope Mark took in his teeth; ran his eye up the long rainspout on the wall; and an instant later gave a spring.

"Take care!" shouted one of the cadets, who saw his purpose. "It's hot!"

Hot? It burned his hands to the bone, but what did Mark care?

Again and again he seized it, again and again with his mighty arms he jerked himself upward, gripping the pipe between his knees, gripping the rope like death, higher and higher!

How the crowd gasped and trembled! He reached the first floor, halfway. He might have climbed that on a ladder, if he had only thought. But it was too late now. On! on! The smoke curled about him and choked him, hid him from view; bright flames leaped out from the seething windows and enveloped him.

"His clothes are afire!" shouted one. "Oh, heavens!"

Out of the smoke he came. Tongues of fire were starting at his trousers, at the end of his coat, getting larger, climbing higher, upon him. And still on he went, his flesh raw, his lungs hot and dry, his strength failing him. And ever about was the fluttering of white, a signal of distress that nerved him to clutch the burning iron yet once again.

Fischer was leaning from the window, straining every nerve, almost hanging by his knees, with outstretched hands. Mallory was climbing, fainting, almost unconscious, still gazing up and gasping. And the crowd could not make a move.

And then an instant later it was over. They saw Fischer give a sudden convulsive clutch beneath him; they saw the gallant plebe totter and sway, cling an instant more, and then, without uttering a sound, plunge downward like a flaming shot and strike with a thud upon the mattress below. But Fischer held the rope!

CHAPTER XXIX

THE FRUITS OF VICTORY

Grace Fuller was safe then, and everybody knew it. But somehow that crowd did not give a single cheer; in fact, every one seemed to have forgotten that she and Fischer were there, and all made a rush for Mallory.

Fischer fastened the rope inside the building, wrapped it about his wrist, took the unconscious figure in his one free arm, and slid swiftly down to safety, just in time to see the flames that threatened Mallory extinguished by the cadets. Grace Fuller was unconscious, so she knew nothing of this, but Fischer did, and he staggered over toward the gallant plebe.

"How is he?" he cried. "How is he? Don't tell me he's——"

Fischer hated to say the word, but as he stared at the motionless figure he feared that it was true, that Mallory had given his life for his friends.

A surgeon was at his side an instant later, bending over the prostrate form—Mallory was unconscious and nearly dead from exhaustion and pain alone. His legs were burned to a blister, his hands were a sight to make one sick. As to the fall, who could say? The surgeon shook his head sadly as he got up and called for a stretcher to carry the lad down to the hospital.

That incident once past the battalion turned its energies to extinguishing the flames. But they were listless and careless energies for some reason. There seemed to be something on the battalion's mind.

A guilty conscience is a poor companion for any work. And the thought of Mallory and what he had done, and what they had done to him, gave the cadets a very guilty conscience indeed.

Those who had taken part in that beating were the most worried and unhappy of all, for they had done something they might never be able to atone for. They seemed to hear those words of Mallory's—and they thought of how true they had come—"Some day I may have a chance to show you how much of a coward I am."

They got the fire out entirely in an hour or two, and then sadly the corps marched back to the silent camp. There was a noticeable lack of satisfaction one might have expected to see after the weary task was so creditably performed. The thought of Mallory was a weight of lead upon the heart of every one. That plebe had suddenly become the one object of all the hopes and prayers of the corps.

Groups of silent lads gathered about the tents, conversing in low and subdued whispers when they said anything at all. The picture of Mallory's figure clinging to the side of that burning house was before their eyes every moment. Fischer had told them the story of Mallory's reasons for daring their wrath, and his news put the plebe's action in quite a different light. It made the cadets yet more remorseful for their cruelty.

George Elliot has remarked that "when Death, the great Reconciler comes, it is not our leniency, but our harshness we repent of."

The drug sounded taps a few minutes later for the second time that night. The cadets scattered silently to their tents, realizing that they would have to wait until the morrow to get tidings of poor Mallory's fate.

It seemed, however, that West Point's interest in the matter was so great that even military rules could not stand before it. The cadets had scarcely fallen asleep again, before several members of the guard went from tent to tent with the glad tidings from the hospital that Cadet Mallory and Miss Grace Fuller were conscious and would surely recover. And the news was sent by order of Lieutenant Allen himself.

Two days later Mark was lying upon a bed in the cadet hospital. We would scarcely have known Mark, to look at him; his face was pale and his arm trembled when he moved it. But Mark was happy for all that.

He was reaping the fruits of his bravery, then. He was still in pain, it is true; any one who has ever blistered one's finger with fire may be able to imagine the feelings Mark got from those two bandaged hands of his. But he had forgotten all about that for a time.

The reason for that is not far to seek. The sunlight as it streamed into that room was reflected from a wealth of golden hair that in turn lit up Mark's pale features. It was Grace Fuller who was sitting by his bedside; and Grace Fuller was trying to thank him for what he had done for her.

Her tone was low and earnest as she spoke:

"Mark," she said—"I have never called you Mark before, but I will now, if you will let me—the debt I owe to you I can never repay; but if true friendship is anything you may have that. That is all I can give."

Mark answered nothing; but he gazed at the girl earnestly.

"This is the second time," continued she, "that you have been in this hospital for me. I do not know what others think of it, but I know that I shall never forget it as long as I live."

Concerning what others thought, Grace was very speedily to learn. It is necessary to interrupt her thankful words, for just then an unpoetic attendant came into the room.

"Mr. Mallory," said he, "there are some cadets outside who want to see you. The surgeon says that they may——"

"Send them in," said Mark, weakly. And then he added to Grace, with a faint attempt at a smile: "I wonder if they want me to fight."

Grace said nothing to that, but her eyes flashed for a moment. She had heard the story of how the cadets had treated Mark, and she had made up her mind that if they had anything more to say about cowardice she was going to take a hand. Grace Fuller had her own ideas on the subject of cowards.

The cadets entered the room a moment later, and when Mark glanced at them he started with no little surprise. It was the committee from the first class, the same committee that had been taunting him a few days previously.

"Well, gentlemen?" said Mark, inquiringly.

Evidently the cadets had an embarrassing task before them. They had sidled into the room rather awkwardly, all the more so when they espied Grace Fuller's beautiful face, which was all the more beautiful for its present paleness.

Once in the room they had backed up against the wall, eying the two uneasily.

"Ahem!" said the spokesman.

"Well?" inquired Mark again.

By way of answer the spokesman took from beneath his jacket a folded paper. This he opened before him with some solemnity.

"Mr. Mallory," he began—"ahem! I have been appointed, together with my two classmates here, to—er—convey to you the following notice from the first class."

Here the spokesman stopped abruptly and shifted uneasily. Mark bowed, as well as he could under the circumstances.

"This letter," continued the cadet, "is from the president of the class. Listen, please:

"'Cadet Mallory, West Point:

"'Dear Sir: As president of the first class of the corps of cadets I have the duty and pleasure of submitting to you the following set of resolutions adopted unanimously by the class at a meeting held this morning.

"'Respectfully Yours,
"'George T. Fischer,
"'Cadet Captain, Company A.'"

After that imposing document the spokesman paused for breath. Mark waited in silence. When the cadet thought that there had been suspense enough for so important an occasion he raised the paper and continued:

"'Whereas—
"'Cadet Mallory of the fourth class has performed before the whole academy an act of heroism and self-sacrifice which merits immediate and signal recognition.
"'Resolved—
"'That the class hereby desires, both as a class and as individuals, to offer to Cadet Mallory their sincere apology

for all offensive remarks addressed to him under any circumstances whatsoever.

"'That the class hereby expresses the greatest regret for all attacks made by it upon Cadet Mallory.

"'That the class hereby extends to Cadet Mallory its assurance of respect.

"'And that the president of the class be requested to forward a copy of these resolutions to Cadet Mallory at once.'"

At the close of this most imposing document the young cadet folded the paper and put it away, then gazed at Mark with a what-more-do-you-want? sort of air. As for Mark, he was lying back on his pillow gazing into space and thinking.

"That's pretty decent," he observed, meditatively; then he raised himself up and gazed at the three quizzically.

"Tell the first class," said he, "that I cannot make much of a speech, but that I accept their apology with the same sincerity it's given. I thank them for their regards, and also for having released me from my fighting obligations. And now," he added, "since this appears to be a time of mutual brotherly love, concession and reciprocity, I don't mind taking a share myself. Tell the class that it's very probable that when I join them again— —"

Here Mark paused in order to let his important announcement have due weight.

"I'll try to be a little less B. J. Good-afternoon."

"Say, that letter's great!" cried Texas, when he heard of it. "Whoop! I almost feel like hurrahing for them old first classers."

"It's very nice," said the Parson. "Yea, by Zeus, it's all right."

"Couldn't do less, b'gee!" cried Dewey. "Mark shamed 'em all, b'gee."

And the Banded Seven agreed—just as they always did.

THE END